PRAISE FOR
ALISTAIR MacLEAN's
SAN ANDREAS

"MacLean at his unholy best, ripping our nerves, combining tragedy with dread as we race on, armchair victims of an overdose of shock."

Los Angeles Times

"Combines high-seas action with a process-of-elimination mystery in the sort of thriller his fans have come to expect."

St. Louis Post-Dispatch

"Nail-biting scrapes and absorbing sleuthing keep the pages turning . . . with a dash of romance, a pinch of sentiment, and lots of manly grit."

Booklist

"MacLean's knowledge of the workings of a ship in wartime is remarkable, and he communicates it with a gripping excitement."

Mystery News

Also by Alistair MacLean
Published by Fawcett Books:

H.M.S. ULYSSES
SOUTH BY JAVA HEAD
THE SECRET WAYS
NIGHT WITHOUT END
FEAR IS THE KEY
ICE STATION ZEBRA
WHEN EIGHT BELLS TOLL
WHERE EAGLES DARE
THE GUNS OF NAVARONE
PUPPET ON A CHAIN
THE SATAN BUG
THE BLACK SHRIKE
CARAVAN TO VACCARES
BEAR ISLAND
THE WAY TO DUSTY DEATH
BREAKHEART PASS
CIRCUS
THE GOLDEN RENDEZVOUS
THE GOLDEN GATE
GOODBYE CALIFORNIA
SEAWITCH
FORCE 10 FROM NAVARONE
ATHABASCA
RIVER OF DEATH
PARTISANS
FLOODGATE
SAN ANDREAS
THE LONELY SEA

ALISTAIR MacLEAN

SANTORINI

FAWCETT CREST • NEW YORK

Dave

To
Tom and Rena

SANTORINI

1

An overhead broadcaster on the bridge of the frigate *Ariadne* crackled into life, a bell rang twice and then O'Rourke's voice came through, calm, modulated, precise and unmistakably Irish. O'Rourke was commonly referred to as the weatherman, which he wasn't at all.

"Just picked up an odd-looking customer. Forty miles out, bearing two-two-two."

Talbot pressed the reply button. "The skies above us, Chief, are teeming with odd-looking customers. At least six airlines crisscross this patch of the Aegean. NATO planes, as you know better than all of us, are all around us. And those pesky fighter-bombers and fighters from the Sixth Fleet are all around."

"Ah! But this is a very odd odd-looking lad."

O'Rourke's voice was unruffled as ever, unmoved by the less than flattering reference to the Sixth Fleet, from which he was on temporary loan. "No trans-Aegean airline uses the flight path this plane is on. There are no NATO planes in this particular sector on my display screen. And the Americans would have let us know. A very courteous lot, Captain. The Sixth Fleet, I mean."

"True, true." The Sixth Fleet, Talbot was aware, would have informed him of the presence of any of their aircraft in his vicinity, not from courtesy but because regulations demanded it, a fact of which O'Rourke was as well aware as he was. O'Rourke was a doughty defender of his home fleet. "That all you have on this lad?"

"No. Two things. This plane is on a due south-west-to-northeast course. I have no record, no information of any plane that could be following this course. Secondly, I'm pretty sure it's a big plane. We should see in about four minutes—his course is on a direct intersection with ours."

"The size is important, Chief? Lots of big planes around."

"Not at forty-three thousand feet, sir, which is what this one is. Only a Concorde does that and we know there are no Concordes in this area. Military job, I would guess."

"Of unknown origin. A bandit? Could be. Keep an eye on him." Talbot looked around and caught the eye of his second-in-command, Lieutenant Commander Van Gelder. Van Gelder was short, very broad, deeply tanned, flaxen-haired, and seemed to find life a source of constant amusement. He was smiling now as he approached the captain.

"Consider it done, sir. The spyglass and a photo for your family album?"

"That's it. Thank you." The *Ariadne* carried an immense and, to the uninitiated, quite bewildering variety of looking and listening instruments that may well have been unmatched by any other naval ship afloat. Among those instruments was what Van Gelder had referred to as the spyglass. This was a combined telescope and camera, invented and built by the French, of the type used by spy satellites in orbit, which was capable, under ideal atmospheric circumstances, of locating and photographing a white plate from an altitude of two hundred and fifty miles. The focal length of the telescope was almost infinitely adjustable: in this case Van Gelder would probably use a one-in-a-hundred resolution, which would have the optical effect of bringing the intruder— if intruder it was—to an apparent altitude of four hundred feet. In the cloudless July skies of the Cyclades this presented no problem at all.

Van Gelder had just left the bridge when another loudspeaker came to life, the repeated double buzzer identifying it as the radio room. The helmsman, Leading Seaman Harrison, leaned forward and made the appropriate switch.

"I have an SOS. I think—repeat, think—vessel's position is just south of Thera. All I have. Very garbled, certainly not a trained operator. Just keeps repeating "Mayday, Mayday, Mayday." Myers, the radio operator on duty, sounded annoyed: every radio operator, the tone of his voice said, should be as expert and efficient as he was. "Wait a minute, though." There was a pause, then Myers came on again. "Sinking, he says. Four times he said he was sinking."

Talbot said, "That all?"

"That's all, sir. He's gone off the air."

"Well, just keep listening on the distress frequency, Harrison, oh-nine-oh or near enough. Can't be more than ten, twelve miles away." He reached for the engine control and turned it up to full power. The *Ariadne*, in the modern fashion, had dual engine-room and bridge controls. The engine room customarily had only one rating, a leading stoker, on watch, and this only because custom dictated it, not because necessity demanded it. The lone watchman might, just possible, be wandering around with an oil can in hand but more probably was immersed in one of the lurid magazines with which what was called the engine-room library was so liberally stocked. The *Ariadne*'s chief engineer, Lieutenant McCafferty, rarely ventured near his own domain. A first-class engineer, McCafferty claimed he was allergic to diesel fumes and treated with a knowing disdain the frequently repeated observation that, because of the engine room's highly efficient extractor fans, it was virtually impossible for anyone to detect the smell of diesel. He was to be found that afternoon, as he was most afternoons, seated in a deck chair aft and immersed in his favorite form of relaxation, the reading of detective novels heavily laced with romance of the more dubious kind.

The distant sound of the diesels deepened—the *Ariadne* was capable of a very respectable thirty-five knots—and the bridge began to vibrate quite noticeably. Talbot reached for a phone and got through to Van Gelder.

"We've picked up a distress signal. Ten, twelve miles away. Let me know when you locate this bandit and I'll cut the engines." The spyglass, though splendidly gimballed to deal with the worst vagaries of pitching and rolling, was quite incapable of coping with even the mildest vibration, which, more often than not, produced a very fuzzy photograph.

Talbot moved out onto the port wing to join the lieutenant who stood there, a tall, thin young man with fair hair, thick glasses and a permanently lugubrious expression.

"Well, Jimmy, how do you fancy this? A maybe bandit and a sinking vessel at the same time. Should relieve the tedium of a long, hot summer's afternoon, don't you think?"

The lieutenant looked at him without enthusiasm. Lieutenant the Right Honorable Lord James Denholm—Talbot called him Jimmy for brevity's sake—seldom waxed enthusiastic about anything.

"I don't fancy it at all, Captain." Denholm

waved a languid hand. "Disturbs the even tenor of my ways."

Talbot smiled. Denholm was surrounded by an almost palpable aura of aristocratic exhaustion that had disturbed and irritated Talbot in the early stage of their acquaintanceship, a feeling that had lasted for no more than half an hour. Denholm was totally unfitted to be a naval officer of any kind and his highly defective eyesight should have led to his automatic disbarment from any navy in the world. But Denholm was aboard the *Ariadne* not because of his many connections with the highest echelons of society—heir to an earldom, his blood indisputably the bluest of the blue—but because, without question, he was the right man in the right place. The holder of three scientific degrees—from Oxford, UCLA and MIT, all summa cum laude—in electrical engineering and electronics, Denholm was as close to being an electronics wizard as any man could ever hope to be. Not that Denholm would have claimed to be anything of, as he would have said, the ridiculous kind. Despite his lineage and academic qualifications, Denholm was modest and retiring to a fault. This reticence extended even to the making of protests, which was why, despite his feeble objections—he had been under no compulsion to go—he had been dragooned into the Navy in the first place.

He said to Talbot, "This bandit, Captain—if it is a bandit—what do you intend to do about it?"

"I don't intend to do anything about it."

"But if he *is* a bandit—well, then, he's spying, isn't he?"

"Of course."

"Well, then—"

"What do you expect me to do, Jimmy? Bring him down? Or are you itching to try out this experimental laser gun you have with you?"

Denholm was genuinely horrified. "I've never fired a gun in anger in my life. Correction. I've never even fired a gun."

"If I wanted to bring him down, a teeny-weeny heat-seeking missile would do the job very effectively. But we don't do things like that. We're civilized. Besides, we don't provoke international incidents. An unwritten law."

"Sounds a very funny law to me."

"Not at all. When the United States or NATO play war games, as we are doing now, the Soviets track us very closely indeed, whether on land, sea or air. We don't complain. We can't. When they're playing their games we do exactly the same to them. Can, admittedly, have its awkward moments. Not so long ago, when the U.S. Navy were carrying out exercises in the Sea of Japan, an American destroyer banged into, and quite severely damaged, a Russian submarine which was monitoring things a little too closely."

"And *that* didn't cause what you've just called an international incident?"

"Certainly not. Nobody's fault. Mutual apologies between the two captains and the Russian was towed to a safe port by another Russian warship. Vladivostok, I believe it was." Talbot turned his head. "Excuse me. That's the radio-room call-up."

"Myers again," the speaker said. "*Delos*. Name of the sinking vessel. Very brief message—explosion, on fire, sinking fast."

"Keep listening," Talbot said. He looked at the helmsman, who already had a pair of binoculars to his eyes. "You have it, Harrison?"

"Yes, sir." Harrison handed over the binoculars and twitched the wheel to port. "Fire off the port bow."

Talbot picked it up immediately, a thin black column of smoke rising vertically, unwaveringly, into the blue and windless sky. He was just lowering his glasses when the bell rang twice again. It was O'Rourke, the weatherman, or, more officially, the senior long-range-radar operator.

"Lost him, I'm afraid. The bandit, I mean. I was looking at the vectors on either side of him to see if he had any friends and when I came back he was gone."

"Any ideas, Chief?"

"Well." O'Rourke sounded doubtful. "He *could* have exploded but I doubt it."

"So do I. We've had the spyglass trained on his approach bearing and they'd have picked up an explosion for sure."

"Then he must have gone into a steep dive. A very steep dive. God knows why. I'll find him." The speaker clicked off.

Almost at once a telephone rang again. It was Van Gelder.

"Two-two-two, sir. Smoke. Plane. Could be the bandit."

"Almost certainly is. The weatherman's just lost it off the long-range-radar screen. Probably a waste of time, but try to get that photograph anyway."

He moved out onto the starboard wing and trained his glasses over the starboard quarter. He picked it up immediately, a heavy dark plume of smoke with, he thought, a glow of red at its center. It was still quite high, at an altitude of four or five thousand feet. He didn't pause to check how deeply the plane was diving or whether or not it actually was on fire. He moved quickly back into the bridge and picked up a phone.

"Sublieutenant Cousteau. Quickly." A brief pause. "Henri? Captain. Emergency. Have the launch and the lifeboat slung outboard. Crews to stand by to lower. Then report to the bridge." He rang down to the engine room for "slow ahead," then said to Harrison, "Hard aport. Steer north."

Denholm, who had moved out onto the starboard wing, returned, lowering his binoculars.

"Well, even I can see that plane. Not a plane, rather a huge streamer of smoke. Could that have been the bandit, sir—if it was a bandit?"

"Must have been."

Denholm said, tentatively, "I don't care much for his line of approach, sir."

"I don't care much for it myself, Lieutenant, especially if it's a military plane and even more especially if it's carrying bombs of any sort. If you look, you'll see that we're getting out of its way."

"Ah. Evasive action." Denholm hesitated, then said doubtfully, "Well, as long as he doesn't alter course."

"Dead men don't alter courses."

"That they don't." Van Gelder had just returned to the bridge. "And the man or the men behind the controls of that plane are surely dead. No point in my staying there, sir—Gibson's better with the spyglass camera than I am and he's very busy with it. We'll have plenty of photographs to show you but I doubt whether we'll be able to learn very much from them."

"As bad as that? You weren't able to establish anything?"

"Very little, I'm afraid. I did see the outer engine on the port wing. So it's a four-engine jet. Civil or military, I've no idea."

"A moment, please." Talbot moved out onto the port wing, looked aft, saw that the blazing plane —there was no mistaking the flames now—was due astern, at less than half the height and distance of when he had first seen it, returned to the bridge, told Harrison to steer due north, then turned again to Van Gelder.

"That was all you could establish?"

"About. Except that the fire is definitely located in the nose cone, which would rule out any engine explosion. It couldn't have been hit by a missile, because we know there are no missile-carrying planes around—even if there were, a heat-seeking missile, the only type that could nail it at that altitude, would have gone for the engines, not the nose cone. It could only have been an up-front internal explosion."

Talbot nodded, reached for a phone, asked the exchange for the sick bay and was through immediately.

"Doctor? Would you detail a sick-bay attendant —with first-aid kit—to stand by the lifeboat." He paused for a moment. "Sorry, no time to explain. Come on up to the bridge." He looked aft through the starboard-wing doorway, turned and took the wheel from the helmsman. "Take a look, Harrison. A good look."

Harrison moved out onto the starboard wing, had his good look—it took him only a few seconds—returned and took the wheel again.

"Awful." He shook his head. "They're finished, sir, aren't they?"

"So I would have thought."

"They're going to miss us by at least a quarter mile. Maybe a half." Harrison took another quick look through the doorway. "At this angle of descent, they should land—rather, hit the sea—a mile, mile and a half ahead. Unless by some fluke they carry on and hit the island. That would be curtains, sir."

"It would indeed." Talbot looked ahead through the for'ard screens. Thera Island was some four miles distant, with Cape Akrotiri lying directly to the north and Mount Elias, the highest point of the island—it was close to two thousand feet—to the northeast. Between them, but about five miles further distant, a tenuous column of bluish smoke, hardly visible against a cloudless sky, hung lazily in the air. This marked the site of Thera Village, the only settlement of any size on the island. "But the damage would be limited to the plane. The southwest of the island is barren. I don't think anyone lives there."

"What are we going to do, sir? Stop over the point where it goes down?"

"Something like that. You can handle it yourself. Or maybe another quarter of half mile further on along the line he was taking. Have to wait and see. Fact is, Harrison, I know no more about it than you do. It may disintegrate on impact or, if it survives that, it may carry on some distance underwater. Not for far, I should think—not if its nose has gone. Number One"—this to Van Gelder—"what depths do we have here?"

"I know the five-fathom mark is about half mile offshore along the south of the island. Beyond that, it shelves pretty steeply. I'll have to check in the chart room. At the moment I'd guess we're in two to three hundred fathoms. A sonar check, sir?"

"Please." Van Gelder left, brushing by Sublieutenant Cousteau as he did. Cousteau, barely in his twenties, was happy-go-lucky, always eager and willing and a more than competent seaman. Talbot beckoned him out onto the starboard wing.

"Have you seen it, Henri?"

"Yes, sir." Cousteau's normal cheerfulness was in marked abeyance. He gazed in unwilling fascination at the blazing, smoking plane, now directly abeam and at an altitude of under a thousand feet. "What a damn awful thing."

"Aye, it's not nice." They had been joined by Surgeon Lieutenant Commander Andrew Grierson. Grierson was dressed in white shorts and a flowing multicolored Hawaiian shirt, which he doubtless regarded as the correct dress of the day for the summer Aegean. "So this is why you wanted Moss and his first-aid box." Moss was the leading sick-bay attendant. "I'm thinking maybe I should be going myself." Grierson was a West Highland Scot, as was immediately evident from his accent, an accent which he never attempted to conceal, for the excellent reason that he saw no earthly reason why he ever should. "If there are any survivors, which I consider bloody unlikely, I know something about decompression problems, which Moss doesn't."

Talbot was conscious of the heavier vibration beneath his feet. Harrison had increased speed and was edging a little to the east. Talbot didn't even give it a second thought: his faith in his senior quartermaster was complete.

"Sorry, Doctor, but I have more important things for you to do." He pointed to the east. "Look under the trail of smoke to the plane's left."

"I see it. I should have seen it before. Somebody sinking."

"Something called the *Delos*, a private yacht, and, as you say, sinking. Explosion and on fire. Pretty heavily on fire, too, I would think. Burns, injuries."

"The plane's silent, sir," Cousteau said. "The engines have been shut off."

` "Survivors, you think? I'm afraid not. The explosion may have destroyed the controls, in which case the engines shut off automatically."

"Disintegrate or dive?" Grierson said. "Daft question. We'll know all too soon."

Van Gelder joined them. "I make it eighty fathoms here, sir. Sonar says seventy. They're probably right. Doesn't matter, it's shallowing anyway."

Talbot nodded and said nothing. Nobody said anything, nobody felt like saying anything. The plane, or the source of the dense column of smoke, was now less than a hundred feet above the water. Suddenly, the source of the smoke and flame dipped and then was abruptly extinguished. Even then they failed to catch a glimpse of the plane, it had been immediately engulfed in a fifty-foot-high curtain of water and spray. There was no sound of impact and certainly no disintegration, for when the water and the spray cleared away there was only the empty sea and curiously small waves, little more than ripples, radiating outward from the point of impact.

- Talbot touched Cousteau on the arm. "Your cue, Henri. How's the whaler's radio?"

"Tested yesterday, sir. Okay."

"If you find anything, anybody, let us know. I have a feeling you won't need that radio. When we stop, lower away, then keep circling around. We should be back in half an hour or so." Cousteau left and Talbot turned to Van Gelder. "When we stop, tell sonar I want the exact depth."

Five minutes later the whaler was in the water and moving away from the side of the *Ariadne*. Talbot rang for full power and headed east.

Van Gelder hung up a phone. "Thirty fathoms, sonar says. Give or take a fathom."

"Thanks. Doctor?"

"Hundred and eighty feet," Grierson said. "I don't even have to rub my chin over that one. The answer is no. Even if anyone could escape from the fuselage—which I think would be impossible in the first place—they'd die soon after surfacing. Diver's bends. Burst lungs. They wouldn't know that they'd have to breathe out all the way up. A trained, fit submariner, possibly with breathing apparatus, might do it. There would be no fit, trained submariners aboard that plane. Question's academic anyway. I agree with you, Captain. The only men aboard that plane are dead men."

Talbot nodded and reached for a phone.

"Myers? Signal to General Carson. Unidentified four-engine plane crashed in sea two miles south of Cape Akrotiri, Thera Island. 1415 hours. Impossible to determine whether military or civilian. First located altitude forty-three thousand feet. Apparent cause internal explosion. No further details available at present. No NATO planes reported in vicinity. Have you any information? Sylvester. Send Code B."

"Wilco, sir. Where do I send it?"

"Rome. Wherever he is, he'll have it two minutes later."

Grierson said, "Well, yes, if anyone knows, he should." Carson was the Commander-in-Chief, Southern European NATO. He lifted his binoculars and looked at the vertical column of smoke, now no more than four miles to the east. "A yacht, as you say, and making quite a bonfire. If there's anyone still aboard, they're going to be very warm indeed. Are you going alongside, Captain?"

"Alongside." Talbot looked at Denholm. "What's your estimate of the value of the electronic gear we have aboard?"

"Twenty million. Maybe twenty-five. A lot, anyway."

"There's your answer, Doctor. That thing's gone bang once already. It can go bang once again. I am not going alongside. *You* are. In the launch. That's expendable. The *Ariadne*'s not."

"Well, thank you very much. And what intrepid soul—"

"I'm sure Number One here will be delighted to ferry you across."

"Ah. Number One, have your men wear overalls, gloves and flash masks. Injuries from burning diesel can be very unpleasant indeed." Grierson paused and shrugged. "I go to prepare myself for self-immolation."

16

"And don't forget your life belts." Grierson didn't deign to answer.

They had halved the remaining distance to the burning yacht when Talbot got through to the radio room again.

"Message dispatched?"

"Dispatched and acknowledged."

"Anything more from the *Delos*?"

"Nothing."

"Delos," Denholm said. "That's about eighty miles north of here. Alas, the Cyclades will never be the same for me again." Denholm sighed. Electronics specialist or not, he regarded himself primarily as a classicist and, indeed, he was totally fluent in speaking, reading and writing both Latin and Greek. He was deeply immersed in their ancient cultures, as the considerable library in his cabin bore testimony. He was also much given to quotations and he quoted now.

"The isles of Greece, the isles of Greece!
　　Where burning Sappho loved and sung,
　Where grew the arts of war and peace,
　　Where Delos rose, and Phoebus sprung,
　Eternal summer—"

"Your point is taken, Lieutenant," Talbot said. "We'll cry tomorrow. In the meantime, let us address ourselves to the problem of those poor souls on the fo'c'sle. I count five of them."

"So do I." Denholm lowered his glasses. "What's all the frantic waving for? Surely to God they can't imagine we haven't seen them?"

"They've seen us, all right. Relief, Lieutenant.

17

Expectation of rescue. But there's more to it than that. A certain urgency in their waving. A primitive form of semaphoring. What they're saying is 'Get us the hell out of here and be quick about it.'"

"Maybe they're expecting another explosion?"

"Could be that. Harrison, I want to come to a stop on their starboard beam. At, you understand, a prudent distance."

"A hundred yards, sir?"

"Fine."

The *Delos* was—or had been—a rather splendid yacht. A streamlined eighty-footer, it was obvious that it had been, until very, very recently, a dazzling white. Now, because of a combination of smoke and diesel oil, it was mainly black. A rather elaborate superstructure consisted of a bridge, a saloon, a dining room and what may or may not have been a galley. The still dense smoke and flames rising six feet above the poop deck indicated the source of the fire—almost certainly the engine room. Just aft of the fire a small motorboat was still secured to its davits: it wasn't difficult to guess that either the explosion or the fire had rendered it inoperable.

Talbot said, "Rather odd, don't you think, Lieutenant?"

"Odd?" Denholm said carefully.

"Yes. You can see that the flames are dying away. One would have thought that would reduce the danger of further explosion." Talbot moved out onto the port wing. "And you will have observed that the water level is almost up to the deck."

"I can see she's sinking."

"Indeed. If you were aboard a vessel that was either going to go up or drag you down when it sank, what would your natural reaction be?"

"To be elsewhere, sir. But I can see that their motorboat has been damaged."

"Agreed. But a craft that size would carry alternative lifesaving equipment. If not a Carley float, then certainly an inflatable rubber dinghy. And any prudent owner would carry a sufficiency of life belts and life jackets for the passengers and crew. I can even see two life belts in front of the bridge. But they haven't done the obvious thing and abandoned ship. I wonder why."

"I've no idea, sir. But it is damned odd."

"When we've rescued those distressed mariners and brought them aboard, you, Jimmy, will have forgotten how to speak Greek."

"But I will not have forgotten how to listen in Greek?"

"Precisely."

"Commander Talbot, you have a devious and suspicious mind."

"It goes with the job, Jimmy. It goes with the job."

Harrison brought the *Ariadne* to a stop off the starboard beam of the *Delos* at the agreed hundred-yard distance. Van Gelder was away in the launch at once and was very quickly alongside the fo'c'sle of the *Delos*. Two boat hooks around the guardrail stanchions held them in position. As the launch and the bow of the sinking yacht were now almost level, it took only a few seconds to transfer the six survivors—another had joined the group of five that Talbot had seen —aboard the launch. They were, indeed, a sorry and sadly bedraggled lot, so covered in diesel and smoke that it was quite impossible to discriminate among them on the basis of age, six or nationality.

Van Gelder said, "Any of you here speak English?"

"We all do." The speaker was short and stocky and that was all that could be said of him in the way of description. "Some of us just a little. But enough." The voice was heavily accented but readily understood. Van Gelder looked at Grierson.

"Any of you injured, any of you burnt?" Grierson said. All shook their heads or mumbled a negative. "Nothing here for me, Number One. Hot showers, detergents, soap. Not to mention a change of clothing."

"Who's in charge here?" Van Gelder asked.

"I am." It was the same man.

"Anybody left aboard?"

"Three men, I'm afraid. They won't be coming with us."

"You mean they're dead?" The man nodded. "I'll check."

"No, no!" His oil-soaked hand gripped Van Gelder's arm. "It is too dangerous, far too dangerous. I forbid it."

"You forbid me nothing." When Van Gelder

wasn't smiling, which wasn't often, he could assume a very discouraging expression indeed. The man withdrew his hand. "Where are those men?"

"In the passageway between the engine room and the stateroom aft. We got them out after the explosion but before the fire began."

"Riley," Van Gelder said to a leading seaman, "come aboard with me. If you think the yacht's going, give me a call." He picked up a torch and was about to board the *Delos* when a hand holding a pair of goggles reached out and stopped him. Van Gelder smiled. "Thank you, Doctor. I hadn't thought of that."

Once aboard he made his way aft and descended the after companionway. There was smoke down there, but not too much, and with the aid of his torch he had no difficulty in locating the three missing men, all huddled shapelessly in a corner. To his right was the engine-room door, slightly buckled from the force of the explosion. Not without some difficulty, he forced the door open and at once began coughing as the foul-smelling smoke caught his throat and eyes. He pulled on the goggles but still there was nothing to see except the red embers of a dying fire emanating from some unknown source. He pulled the door to behind him—reasonably certain there was nothing for him to see in the engine-room anyway—and stopped to examine the three dead men. They were far from being a pretty sight but he forced himself to carry out as thorough an investigation as he could. He spent some quite considerable time bent over the third man—in the circumstances thirty seconds was a long time—and when he straightened he looked both puzzled and thoughtful.

The door to the after stateroom opened easily. There was some smoke there but not so much that he had to use his goggles. The cabin was luxuriously furnished and immaculately tidy, a condition which Van Gelder very rapidly altered. He pulled a sheet from one of the beds, spread it on the floor, opened up wardrobes and drawers, scooped up armfuls of clothes—there was no time to make any kind of selection, and even if there had been he would have been unable to pick and choose, they were all women's clothing —dumped them on the sheet, tied up the four corners, lugged the bundle up the companionway and handed it over to Riley.

"Put this in the launch. I'm going to have a quick look at the for'ard cabins. I think the steps will be at the for'ard end of the saloon under the bridge."

"I think you should hurry, sir."

Van Gelder didn't answer. He had noticed the sea already beginning to trickle over onto the upper deck. Passing into the saloon, he found the companionway at once and descended to a central passage.

He switched on his torch—there was, of course, no electrical power left. There were doors on both sides and one at the end. The first door to port opened up into a food store, the corresponding door to starboard was locked. Van Gelder didn't bother with it: the *Delos* didn't look like the kind of craft that would lack a commodious liquor store. Behind the other doors lay four cabins and two bathrooms. All were empty. As he had done before, Van Gelder spread out a sheet—in the passageway this time—threw some more armfuls of clothes onto it, secured the corners and hurried up on deck.

The launch was no more than thirty yards away when the *Delos*, still on even keel, slid gently under the surface of the sea. There was nothing dramatic to mark its going—just a stream of air bubbles that became gradually smaller and ceased altogether after about twenty seconds.

Talbot was on deck when the launch brought back the six survivors. He looked in concern at the woebegone and bedraggled figures before him.

"My goodness, what a state you people are in. This the lot, Number One?"

"Those that survived, sir. Three died. Impossible to get their bodies out in time." He indicated the figure nearest him. "This is the owner."

"Andropulous," the man said. "Spyros Andropulous. You are the officer in charge?"

"Commander Talbot. My commiserations, Mr. Andropulous."

"And my thanks, Commander. We are very deeply grateful—"

"With respect, sir, that can wait. First things first, and the very first thing is to get yourselves

23

cleaned up immediately. And changed. A problem. Clothes. We'll find some."

"Clothing, we have," Van Gelder said. He pointed at the two sheet-wrapped packages. "Ladies. Gentlemen."

"A mention in dispatches for that, Number One. You said 'ladies'?"

"Two, Commander," Andropulous said. He looked at the two people standing by him. "My niece and her friend."

"Ah. Well, I should apologize, I suppose, but difficult to tell in the circumstances."

"My name is Charial." The voice was unmistakably feminine. "Irene Charial. This is my friend Eugenia."

"We could have met under happier circumstances. Lieutenant Denholm here will take you to my cabin. That bathroom is small but adequate. By the time you bring them back, Lieutenant, I trust they will be recognizable for what they are." He turned to a burly, dark-haired figure who, like most of the crew, wore no insignia of rank. "Chief Petty Officer McKenzie." McKenzie was the senior NCO on the *Ariadne*. "The four gentlemen here, Chief. You know what to do."

"Right away, sir. If you will come with me, gentlemen."

Grierson also left, and Van Gelder and Talbot were left alone. "We can find this place again?" Van Gelder asked.

"No trouble." Talbot looked at him speculatively and pointed toward the northwest. "I've taken a bearing on the monastery and radar station on Mount Elias there. Sonar says that we're in eighteen fathoms. Just to make sure, we'll drop a marker buoy."

General Carson laid down the slip of paper he had been studying and looked at the colonel seated across the table from him.

"What do you make of this, Charles?"

"Could be nothing. Could be important. Sorry, that doesn't help. I have a feeling I don't like it. It would help a bit if we had a sailor around."

Carson smiled and pressed a button. "Do you know if Vice Admiral Hawkins is in the building?"

"He is, sir." A girl's voice. "Do you wish to speak to him or see him?"

"See him, Jean. Ask him if he would be kind enough to stop by."

Vice Admiral Hawkins was very young for one of his rank. He was short, a little overweight, more than a little rubicund as to his features, and exuded an aura of cheerful bonhomie. He didn't look very bright, yet he was widely regarded as having one of the most brilliant minds in the Royal Navy. He took the seat to which Carson had gestured him and glanced at the message slip.

"I see, I see." He laid the message down. "But you didn't ask me here to comment on a perfectly straightforward signal. Sylvester is one of the code names for the frigate HMS *Ariadne*. One of the vessels under your command, sir."

"Don't rub it in, David, I know it, of course—more accurately, I know of it. Don't forget, I'm just a simple landlubber. Odd name, isn't it? Royal Navy ship with a Greek name."

"Courtesy gesture to the Greeks, sir. We're carrying out a joint hydrographic survey with them."

"Is that so?" General Carson ran a hand through his grizzled hair. "I was not aware that I was in the hydrographic business, David."

"You're not, sir, although I have no doubt it could carry out such a survey if it were called for. The *Ariadne* has a radio system that can transmit to, and receive transmissions from, any quarter of the globe. It has telescopes and optical instruments that can pick out the salient features of, say, any passing satellite, even those in geosynchronous orbit—and that's twenty-two thousand miles up. It carries long-range and surface radar that is as advanced as any in the world. And it has a sonar location and detection system that can pick up a sunken object at the bottom of the oceans just as easily as it can pinpoint a lurking submarine. The *Ariadne*, sir, is the eyes and the ears and the voice of your fleet."

"That's nice to know, I must say. Very reassuring. The ability of the commanding officer of the *Ariadne* is—ah—commensurate with this extraordinary array of devices he controls?"

"Indeed, sir. For an exceptionally complex task, an exceptionally qualified man. Commander Talbot is an outstanding officer. Handpicked for the job."

"Who picked him?"

"I did."

"I see. That terminates this line of conversation very abruptly." Carson pondered briefly. "I think, Colonel, that we should ask General Simpson about this one." Simpson, the overall commander of NATO, was the only man who outranked Carson in Europe.

"Don't see what else we can do, sir."

"You would agree, David?"

"No, General. I think you'd be wasting your time. If you don't know anything about this, then I'm damned sure General Simpson doesn't know anything either. This is not an educated guess, call it a completely uneducated guess, but I have an odd feeling that this is one of your planes, sir —an American plane. A bomber, almost certainly, perhaps not yet off the secret lists—it was, after all, flying at an uncommon height."

"The *Ariadne* could have been in error."

"The *Ariadne* does not make mistakes. My job and my life on it." The flat, unemotional voice carried complete conviction. "Commander Talbot is not the only uniquely qualified man aboard. There are at lease thirty others in the same category. We have, for example, an electronics officer so unbelievably advanced in his specialty that none of your much-vaunted high-technology whiz kids in Silicon Valley would even begin to know what he's talking about."

Carson raised a hand. "Point taken, David, point taken. So, an American bomber. A very special bomber because it must be carrying a very special cargo. What would you guess that to be?"

Hawkins smiled faintly. "I am not yet in the ESP business, sir. People or goods. Very secret, very important goods or very secret, very important people. There's only one source that can give you the answer and it might be pointed out that their refusal to divulge this information might put the whole future of NATO at risk and that the individual ultimately responsible for the negative decision would be answerable directly to the President of the United States. One does not imagine that the individual concerned would remain in a position of responsibility for very much longer."

Carson sighed. "If I may speak in a spirit of complaint, David, I might point out that it's easy for you to talk and even easier to talk tough. You're a British officer. I'm an American."

"I appreciate that, sir."

Carson looked at the colonel, who remained silent for a couple of moments, then nodded, slowly, twice. Carson reached for the button on his desk.

"Jean?"

"Sir?"

"Get me the Pentagon. Immediately."

2

"You are unhappy, Vincent?" Vincent was Van Gelder's first name. There were three of them seated in the wardroom, Talbot, Van Gelder and Grierson.

"Puzzled, you might say, sir. I don't understand why Andropulous and the others didn't abandon ship earlier. I saw two inflatable dinghies aboard. Rolled up, admittedly, but those things can be opened and inflated from their gas cylinders in seconds. There were also life belts and life jackets. There was no need for this the-boy-stood-on-the-burning-deck act. They could have left at any time. I'm not saying they'd have been sucked down with the yacht but they might have had a rather uncomfortable time."

"Same thought had occurred to me. Mentioned

it to Andrew here." Talbot nodded to Grierson. "Odd. Maybe Andropulous had a reason. Anything else?"

"The owner tried to stop me from boarding the yacht. Maybe he was concerned with my health. I have the feeling he wasn't. Then I would much like to know what caused that explosion in the engine room. A luxurious yacht like that must have carried an engineer—we can find that out easily enough—and it's a fair guess that the engines would have been maintained in an immaculate condition. I don't see how they could have caused an explosion. We'll have to ask McCafferty about that one."

"That, of course, is why you were so anxious that we pinpoint the spot where the *Delos* went down. You think an expert on the effects of explosives could identify and locate the cause of the explosion? I'm sure he could, especially if he was an expert at determining the causes of aircraft lost through explosions—those people are much better at that sort of thing than the Navy is. Explosives experts we have aboard but no experts on the effects of explosives. Even if we didn't have any divers aboard—well, you and myself apart—trained to work at levels below a hundred feet. We could borrow one easily enough from a lifting vessel or salvage tug but the chances are high that he'd know nothing about explosives. But there's really no problem. It would be a simple matter for any lifting vessel to raise an aircraft fuselage to the surface." Talbot regarded Van

Gelder thoughtfully. "But there's something else worrying you, isn't there?"

"Yes, sir. The three dead men aboard the *Delos* —well, to be specific, just one of them. That's why I asked the doctor here to come along. The three of them were so smoke-begrimed and blackened that it was difficult to tell what they were wearing but two of them appeared to be dressed in white while the third was in a navy-blue overall. An engineer wouldn't wear whites. Well, I admit our engineer, Lieutenant McCafferty, is a dazzling exception; but he's a unique case, he never goes near his engines anyway. In any event, I assumed the man in the overalls was the engineer and he was the one who caught my attention. He had a vicious gash on the back of his head as if he had been blown backward against a very hard, very sharp object."

Grierson said, "Or been struck by a very hard, sharp object?"

"Either way, I suppose. I wouldn't know. I'm afraid I'm a bit weak on the forensic side."

"Had his occiput been crushed?"

"Back of his head? No. At least I'm reasonably certain it hadn't been. I mean, it would have given, wouldn't it, or been squashy? It wasn't like that."

"A blow like that should have caused massive bruising. Did you see any?"

"Difficult to say. He had fairly thick hair. But it was fair. No, I don't think there was any."

"Had it bled a lot?"

"He hadn't bled at all. I'm quite sure of that."

"You didn't notice any holes in his clothing?"

"Not that I could see. He hadn't been shot, if that's what you're asking, and that's what I think you are asking. Who would want to shoot a dead man? His neck was broken."

"Indeed?" Grierson seemed unsurprised. "Poor man was through the wars, wasn't he?"

Talbot said, "What do you think, Andrew?"

"I don't know what to think. The inflicting of the wound on the head and the snapping of the vertebrae could well have been simultaneous. If the two weren't simultaneous, then it could equally well have been—as Vincent clearly seems to think—a case of murder."

"Would an examination of the corpse help at all?"

"It might. I very much doubt it. But an examination of engine-room bulkheads would."

"To see if there were any sharp edges or protrusions that could have caused such a head wound?" Grierson nodded. "Well, when—and if—we ever raise that hull, we should be able to kill two birds with one stone: to determine the causes of both the explosion and this man's death."

"Maybe three birds," Van Gelder said. "It would be interesting to know the number and layout of the fuel tanks in the engine room. There are, I believe, two common layouts—in one case there is just one main fuel tank, athwartship and attached to the for'ard bulkhead, with a generator

or generators on one side of the engine and bat-
teries on the other, plus a water tank to port and
another to starboard; or there could be a fuel tank
on either side with the water tank up front. In
that case the two fuel tanks are interconnected to
keep the fuel levels equal and maintain equilib-
rium."

"A suspicious mind, Number One," Talbot said.
"Very suspicious. What you would like to find, of
course, is just one fuel tank, because you think
Andropulous is going to claim that he didn't
abandon ship because he thought another fuel
tank was about to go and he didn't want his precious passengers splashing about in a sea of blazing fuel oil, which would, of course, also have
destroyed the rubber dinghies."

"I'm grieved, sir. I thought I'd thought of that
first."

"You did, in fact. When the passengers are
cleaned up, see if you can get this young lady
Irene Charial alone and find out if she knows anything about the layout of the engine room. The
casual approach, Vincent, the innocent and cherubic expression, although the latter is probably
beyond you. Anyway, it's possible she's never been
there and knows nothing about it."

"It's equally possible, sir, that she knows all
about it and may well choose to tell me nothing.
Miss Charial is Andropulous's niece."

"The thought had occurred. However, if Andropulous is not all he might be, then the
chances are high that there is some other

member of his ship's company in his confidence and I would have thought that would be a man. I don't say that's because you know what the Greeks are like, because I don't know what the Greeks are like. And we mustn't forget that Andropulous may be as innocent as the driven snow and there may be a perfectly rational explanation for all that has happened. Anyway, it would do no harm to try and you never can tell, Vincent—she might turn out to be a classic Greek beauty."

From the fact that the whaler was lying stopped in the water and Cousteau, his hand resting idly on the tiller, appeared to be expressing no great degree of interest in anything, it was obvious that his wait had been a vain one, a fact he confirmed on his arrival on the bridge.

Talbot called the sonar room. "You have pinpointed the location of the plane?"

"Yes, sir. We're sitting exactly above it. Depth registered is eighteen fathoms. That's the echo from the top of the fuselage. Probably lying in about eighteen fathoms. It's lying in the same direction as it was flying when it came down—northeast to southwest. Picking up some rather odd noises down here, sir. Would you care to come down?"

"Yes, I will." For reasons best known to himself, Halzman, the senior sonar operator, preferred not to discuss it over an open line. "A minute or two." He turned to Van Gelder. "Have McKenzie put down a marker buoy, about midships. Tell him to lower the weight gently. I don't want to bump too hard against the plane's fuselage in case we do actually come into contact with it. When that's been done, I want to anchor. Two anchors. A stern anchor to the northwest, about a hundred yards distant from the buoy, then a bow anchor a similar distance to the southeast."

"Yes, sir. May I suggest the other way around?"

"Of course, you're right. I'd forgotten about our old friend. Taking a holiday today, isn't it? The other way around, of course." The "old friend" to which he referred and which Van Gelder clearly had in mind was the Meltemi wind, referred to as the "Etesian" in the British sailing directions. In the Cyclades, in the summer months—and indeed in most of the Aegean—it blew steadily, but usually only in the afternoon and early evening, from the northwest. If it did start up, the *Ariadne* would ride more comfortably if it were riding into it.

Talbot went to the sonar room, which was only one deck down and slightly aft. The sonar room was heavily insulated against all outside noise and dimly lit by subdued yellow lighting. There were three display screens, two sets of control panels and, over and above all, a considerable number of heavily padded earphones. Halzman caught sight of him in an overhead mirror—there were a number of such mirrors around—removed his earphones and gestured to the seat beside him. Speaking as well as any other kind of sound was kept to a minimum in the sonar room.

"Those earphones, sir. I thought you might be interested in listening for a moment."

Talbot sat and clamped the earphones on. After about fifteen seconds he removed them and turned to Halzman, who had also removed his.

"I can't hear a damned thing."

"With respect, sir, when I said a minute, I meant just that. A minute. First of all you have to listen until you hear the silence, then you'll hear it."

"Whatever that means, I'll try it." Talbot listened again, and just before the allotted minute was up, he leaned forward and creased his brow. After another thirty seconds he removed the headset.

"A ticking sound. Strange, Halzman, you were right. First you hear the silence and then you hear it. Tick . . . tick . . . tick, once every two to three seconds. Very regular. Very faint. You're certain that comes from the plane?"

"I have no doubt, sir."

"Have you ever heard anything like it before?"

"No, sir. I've spent hundreds of hours, more likely thousands, listening to sonar, asdics, hydrophones, but this is something quite new on me."

"I've got pretty good hearing but I had to wait almost a moment before I could imagine I could hear anything. It's very, very faint, isn't it?"

"It is. I had to turn the hearing capacity up to maximum before I stumbled on it—not a practice I would normally follow or recommend—in the wrong circumstances you can get your eardrums blasted off. Why is it so faint? Well, the source of the sound may be very faint to begin with. It's either a mechanical or electrical device. In either case it has to be inside a sealed or waterproof casing. A mechanical device could, of course, operate in water even if it was totally submerged, but operating in water would dampen out the sound almost completely. An electrical device would have to be totally sealed against seawater. The plane's own electrical system, of course, has ceased to function, so it would have to have its own supply system, almost certainly battery-powered. In either event, mechanical or electrical, the sound impulses would have to pass through the waterproof casing, after which it must pass through the fuselage of the plane."

"Have you *any* idea as to what it might be?"

"None whatsoever. It's a two-and-a-half-second sequence—I've timed it. I know of no watch or clock movement that follows that sequence. Do you, sir?"

"No, I don't. You think it could be some sort of timing device?"

"I thought about that, too, sir, but I put it out of my mind." Halzman smiled. "Maybe I'm prejudiced against that idea because of all those cheap and awful video film cassettes we have aboard, with all their special effects and pseudoscience. All I know for sure, sir, is that we have a mysterious plane lying on the seabed there. Lord only knows what kind of mysterious cargo it was carrying."

"Agreed. I think we'd better leave it at that for the moment. Have one of your boys monitor it, once, say, in every fifteen minutes."

When Talbot returned to the bridge he could see the marker buoy just astern, bobbing gently in the very small wake Van Gelder was creating as he edged the *Ariadne* gently to the northwest. Very soon he stopped, juggled the engines to and fro until he reckoned the bows were a hundred yards distant from the buoy, had the anchor dropped, then moved just as slowly astern, the anchor chain being paid out as he went. Soon the stern anchor had been paid out and the *Ariadne* was back to where she had started, the buoy nudging the midships port side.

"Neatly done," Talbot said. "Tell me, Number One, how are you on puzzles?"

"Useless. Even the simplest crossword baffles me."

"No matter. We're picking up a strange noise on the sonar. Maybe you'd like to take a turn along there, perhaps even identify it. Baffles me."

"Consider it done. Back in two or three minutes."

Twenty minutes elapsed before he returned to the bridge, where Talbot was now alone; as the ship was no longer under way, Harrison had retired to his mess.

"That was a long couple of minutes, Vincent, and what are you looking so pleased about?"

"I really don't know how you do it, sir. Incredible. I don't suppose you have any Scottish blood?"

"Not a drop, as far as I'm aware. Am I supposed to be following you, Number One?"

"I thought maybe the second sight. You were right. A classic Greek beauty, Irene. Miss Charial, that is. Odd, mind you, blonde as they come. I thought all those warm-blooded young Latin ladies had hair as black as a raven's wing."

"It's the sheltered life you lead, Vincent. You should go to Andalusia someday. Seville. On one street corner a dusky Moorish maiden, on the next a Nordic blonde. We'll discuss pigmentation some other time. What did you learn?"

"Enough, I hope. It's an art, sir, this casual and inconsequential approach. The questioning, I mean. She seems honest and open enough, not ingenuous, if you know what I mean, but quite straightforward. Certainly didn't give the impression of having anything to hide. Says she doesn't know the engine room well but has been there a couple of times. We came to the question of fuel oil—I was just wondering out loud, natural curiosity, I hope she thought—as to what could have caused the explosion. Seems I was wrong when I said there were just two common ways of arranging fuel and water tanks. Seems there's a third. Two big tanks on either side of the engine, one fuel, one water. How big, I don't know, she was a bit vague about that—no reason why she should know—but at least thousands of liters, she says. If there was a spare fuel tank she didn't know about it. I look forward, sir, to hearing Mr. Andropulous justifying his decision not to abandon ship."

"So do I. Should be interesting. Anyway, congratulations. A good job."

"No hardship, sir." Van Gelder scanned the sea around. "Odd, don't you think, sir? I mean, are we the only ones who heard the SOS? I would have thought the horizon would have been black with converging vessels by this time."

"Not so strange, really. Nearly all the vessels around at this time of year are private yachts and fishermen. Lots of them don't carry any radio at all and even those who do almost certainly wouldn't be permanently tuned to the distress frequency."

"But we are."

"This time I'm ahead of you. The *Delos*—or at least Andropulous—*knew* that we would be permanently tuned to the distress frequency, that we are automatically alerted by bell or buzzer whenever the distress frequency is energized. This presupposes two things. He knew we were a naval vessel and he also knew that we were in the vicinity."

"You realize what you are saying, sir? Sorry, I didn't mean it to sound that way. But the implications, sir. I must say, I really don't like those at all."

"Neither do I. Opens up all sorts of avenues of interesting speculation, doesn't it?" He turned as

McKenzie came onto the bridge. "And how are our oilstained survivors, Chief?"

"Clean, sir. And in dry clothes. I don't think any of them will make the list of the ten best-dressed men." He looked at Van Gelder. "I gather you didn't have too much time, sir, for the selection and careful matching up of clothes. They're a bit of an odd sight, I must say, but respectable enough. I knew you would want to see them, Captain—Mr. Andropulous seems very anxious to see you—and I know you don't like unauthorized people on the bridge, so I took the liberty of putting the four gentlemen and the two young ladies in the wardroom. I hope that's all right, sir."

"Fine. You might ask the surgeon commander and Lieutenant Denholm to join us there. And send a couple of your boys up here to keep a lookout. Who knows, our radar might have a day off."

The six survivors from the *Delos* were standing around rather awkwardly, not talking, when Talbot and Van Gelder reached the wardroom. The four men, as McKenzie had suggested, did present rather an odd spectacle. They looked rather as if they had just raided an old-clothes shop, few of the items of their clothing being a match. In striking contrast, both girls were immaculately clad: dressed in white blouses and white skirts, they could have stepped straight from the pages of *Vogue*.

"Please," Talbot said. "All of you be seated. Before we talk, I suggest we get our priorities right.

41

First things first. You've had a harrowing experience and a lucky escape. I suggest you will not take amiss the suggestion of a suitable restorative." He pressed a bell and a steward entered. "Jenkins. Refreshments. Find out what they would like." Jenkins did so and left.

"I'm the captain," Talbot said. "Talbot. This is Lieutenant Commander Van Gelder. Ah!" The door had opened. "And this is Surgeon Commander Grierson, whom you have met and whose services you fortunately didn't require, and Lieutenant Denholm." He looked at the short stocky man seated before him. "I take it that you, sir, are Mr. Andropulous, the owner."

"I am, Commander, I am." Andropulous had black hair, black eyes, white teeth and a deeply tanned complexion. He looked as if he hadn't shaved that morning, but then, he would always look as if he hadn't shaved that morning. He leapt to his feet, took Talbot's hand and shook it vigorously. He positively radiated a combined aura of benevolence and geniality. "Words cannot express our gratitude. A close-run thing, Commander, a very close-run thing. We owe you our lives."

"I wouldn't go so far as to say that but I'll admit you were in a rather nasty pickle."

"Pickle? Pickle?"

"Dangerous circumstances. I deeply regret your loss of the members of your crew and your yacht."

"The yacht is nothing. I can always buy another. Well, Lloyd's of London can buy it for me.

Sad to lose an old friend like the *Delos* but sadder still, much sadder, to lose the three members of my crew. Been with me for many years. I treasured them all."

"Who were they, sir?"

"My engineer, chef and steward. With me for many years." Andropulous shook his head. "They will be sadly missed."

"Wasn't it odd for a chef and steward to be in the engine room?"

Andropulous smiled sadly. "Not aboard the *Delos*, Commander. It was not exactly run along the lines of a ship of the Royal Navy. They were in the habit of having an after-lunch drink there with the engineer. They had my permission, of course, but they preferred to be discreet about it —and what more discreet place than the engine room? Alas, their discretion cost them their lives."

"That is ironic. May I be introduced to the others?"

"Of course, of course. This is my very dear friend Alexander." Alexander was a tall man with a thin unsmiling face and black cold eyes who didn't look as if he could possibly be anybody's very dear friend. "This is Aristotle, my captain." Andropulous didn't say whether Aristotle was the first or last name; he had watchful eyes and a serious expression but looked like he might, unlike Alexander, be capable of smiling occasionally. "And this is Achmed." He didn't say what occupation Achmed held. He was young, pleasant-faced, and smiled readily. Talbot couldn't even begin to guess at his nationality except that he wasn't Greek.

"But I forget myself. Deplorable, deplorable. I forget myself. Such manners. Should have been ladies first, of course. This is my niece, Irene." Van Gelder hadn't made any mistakes about her, Talbot thought, except that he'd missed out on the wide green eyes and a rather bewitching smile. "And this is Eugenia." This one, Talbot reflected, was much closer to Van Gelder's concept of a warm-blooded young Latin lady. She had a slightly dusky skin, black hair and warm brown eyes. And she also was quite beautiful. It seemed to Talbot that Van Gelder was going to find himself in something of a quandary.

"I congratulate you, Mr. Andropulous," Talbot said gallantly, "and ourselves. Certainly the loveliest passengers we've ever had aboard the *Ariadne*. Ah. The steward."

Andropulous took his glass—a scotch and not a small one—and disposed of half the contents in one gulp.

"My goodness, I needed that. Thank you, Commander, thank you. Not as young as I was, nor as tough either. Age cometh to us all." He quaffed the rest of his drink and sighed.

Talbot said, "Jenkins, another for Mr. Andropulous. A slightly larger measure this time." Jenkins looked at him expressionlessly, closed his eyes momentarily and left.

"The *Ariadne*," Andropulous said. "Rather odd, is it not? Greek name, British vessel."

"Courtesy gesture to your government, sir. We are carrying out a hydrographic charting exercise with your people." Talbot saw no point in mentioning that the *Ariadne* had never carried out a hydrographic exercise in its life and that the ship had been called *Ariadne* to remind the Greeks that it was a multinational vessel and to persuade a wavering Greek government that perhaps NATO wasn't such a bad thing after all.

"Hydrographic, you say? Is that why we're moored fore and aft—a fixed platform for taking bearings?"

"A fixed platform, yes, but in this instance the purpose is not hydrographic. We've had quite a busy afternoon, Mr. Andropulous, and at the moment we're anchored over a plane that crashed into the sea just about the time we were receiving your SOS."

"A plane? Crashed? Good God! What—what kind of plane?"

"We have no idea. It was so wreathed in smoke that it was impossible to distinguish any important features."

"But surely—well, don't you think it was a big plane?"

"It may have been."

"But it could have been a big jet. Maybe *hundreds* of passengers." If Andropulous knew it wasn't a jet carrying hundreds of passengers, his face wasn't saying so.

"It's always possible." Talbot saw no point in telling Andropulous that it was almost certainly a bomber and equally certainly not carrying hundreds of passengers.

"You—you mean to tell me that you left the area to come to our aid?"

"A reasonable enough decision, I think. We were pretty certain that there were people alive aboard the *Delos* and we were also pretty certain that there was no one alive aboard that plane."

"There could have been survivors aboard that plane. I mean, you weren't there to see."

"Mr. Andropulous." Talbot allowed a certain coldness to creep into his voice. "We are, I hope, neither callous nor stupid. Before leaving, we lowered one of our motorboats to circle the area. There were no survivors."

"Oh, dear," Irene Charial said. "Isn't it awful? All those people dead and there we were, busy doing nothing except feeling sorry for ourselves. I'm not being inquisitive, Captain, and I know it's none of my business, but why do you remain anchored here? I mean, there can't possibly be any hope now that some survivors may surface."

"There is no hope, Miss Charial. We're remaining here as a marker until the diving ship arrives."

"But—but it will be too late to save anyone."

"It's already too late, young lady. But they'll send divers down to investigate, to find out whether it's a passenger-carrying jet or not and to try to ascertain the cause of the accident." He was looking, without seeming to look, at Andropulous as he said the last words and felt almost certain that he saw a flicker of expression cross his face.

Andropulous's captain, Aristotle, spoke for the first time. "How deep is this plane, Commander?"

"Seventeen, eighteen fathoms. Just over thirty meters or so."

"Thirty meters," Andropulous said. "Even if they do get inside—and there's no guarantee that they will be able to do so—won't it be difficult to move around and see anything?"

"I can guarantee they'll get inside. There are such things as oxyacetylene torches, you know. And they'll have powerful underwater torches. But they won't bother with either of those things. The divers will carry down a couple of slings with them. A diving ship will have no difficulty at all in bringing the fuselage to the surface. Then they'll be able to examine the plane at their leisure." This time there was no trace of expression on Andropulous's face. Talbot wondered if he, Andropulous, had become aware that such changes in expression were being sought for.

Jenkins entered and handed Talbot a sealed envelope. "From the radio room, sir. Myers said it was urgent."

Talbot nodded, opened the envelope, extracted and read the slip of paper it had held. He slipped it in his pocket and stood.

"My apologies, ladies and gentlemen. I have to go to the bridge. I'll join you at seven o'clock for dinner. Come along with me, Number One."

Once outside, Van Gelder said, "You really are a fearful liar, sir. A fearfully good liar, I mean."

"Andropulous isn't half bad either."

"He's had practice. Between the two of you—well, in his own phrase, it's a close-run thing. Ah, thank you." He unfolded the slip of paper Talbot had handed him. "'Vitally urgent you remain in closest contact with downed plane Stop will join you earliest in the morning Stop Hawkins.' Isn't that the vice admiral, sir?"

"None other. Vitally urgent and flying down to see us. What do you make of that?"

"I make it that he knows something that we don't."

"Indeed. Incidentally, you seem to have forgotten to tell me about your visit to sonar."

"Sorry about that, sir. I had something else on my mind."

"Somebody, not something. Having seen her, I can understand. Well?"

"The noise from the plane? Tick...tick...tick. Could be anything. Halzman half suggested it might be some sort of timing device. Could be that he's right. I don't want to sound alarmist, sir, but I don't think I like it very much."

"I don't particularly care for it myself. Well then, the radio room."

"I thought you said you were going to the bridge?"

"That was for Andropulous's benefit. The less that character knows about anything, the better. I think he's cunning, astute and alert for the slightest nuances."

"Is that why you didn't make any reference to the engine-room explosion?"

"Yes. I may, of course, be doing him a massive injustice."

"You don't really believe that, sir."

"No."

Myers was alone in the radio room. "Another message to Rome," Talbot said. "Again Code B. To Vice Admiral Hawkins. Message received. Strongly advise that you come soonest. Tonight. Report repeated two-and-a-half-second ticking sounds from plane. Could be timing device. Please phone immediately."

"A ticking sound, possibly a timing device, Talbot says." Vice Admiral Hawkins was standing by Carson's chair as the general read and reread the slip of paper Hawkins had just handed him.

"A timing device. We don't have to discuss the implications of this." From his high-rise office Carson looked out over the roofs of Rome, then at the colonel across the desk, then finally up at Hawkins. He pressed a button on his desk.

"Get me the Pentagon."

The Chairman of the Joint Chiefs of Staff was also standing as the man behind the desk read the slip of paper he had just been handed. He read it three times, laid it down carefully on the desk, smoothed it out and looked across at the

Chairman. His face looked drawn and tired and old.

"We know what this means, or what it could mean. If anything goes wrong the international repercussions will be enormous, General."

"I'm afraid I'm fully aware of that, sir. Apart from the universal condemnation, we will become the outcasts of the world."

"And no hint of any Soviet involvement."

"None whatsoever. No proof, direct or indirect. As far as the world is concerned, they are blameless. My first reaction is that they are indeed blameless. My second thoughts are exactly the same. I can see no way they are linked with this. We bear the burden, sir."

"We bear the burden. And will stand condemned before the court of mankind." The general made no reply. "The Chiefs have no suggestions?"

"None that I regard as very useful. In short, bluntly, none. We have to rely on our people out there. Carte blanche, sir?"

"We have no option. How good are your men in the Mediterranean?"

"The very best. No rhetoric, sir. I mean it."

"And this British vessel on the spot?"

"The frigate *Ariadne*? A very special vessel indeed, I am given to understand. Whether or not it can cope with this, no one can say. There are too many imponderables."

"Do we pull it out?"

"That's not for my decision, sir."

"I know it's not." He was silent for a long moment, then said, "It may be our only hope. It stays."

"Yes, Mr. President."

Talbot was alone with Van Gelder on the bridge when the radio room called.

"I have voice contact with Rome, sir. Where will you take it?"

"Here." He gestured to Van Gelder to take up a listening phone. "Talbot here."

"Hawkins. I'm leaving shortly with two civilians for Athens. You'll have a phone call from there letting you know our estimated time of arrival. We'll be landing on Thera Island. Have a launch standing by to meet us."

"Yes, sir. Take a taxi down to Athinio—there's a new wharf about two miles south of the Thera Village anchorage."

"My map shows that the Thera anchorage is nearer."

"What your map may not show is that the only way down to the Thera anchorage is by mule track down a precipitous cliff. A seven-hundred-foot cliff, to be precise."

"Thank you, Talbot. A life saved. You have not forgotten my twin bêtes noires, my fatal flaws. Till this evening, then."

"What bêtes noires?" Van Gelder said. "What flaws?"

"He hates horses. I would imagine the detestation extends to mules. And he suffers from acrophobia."

"That sounds a very nasty thing to suffer from. And what might that be?"

"Vertigo. A fear of heights. Almost got him disbarred from entry to the Navy. He had a powerful aversion to climbing up rigging."

"You know him well, then?"

"Pretty well. Now, this evening. I'd normally send young Henri to pick anybody up, but Vice Admiral Hawkins and the two no doubt equally distinguished civilians who are with him are not anybody. So we do it in style. A Lieutenant Commander, I thought."

"My pleasure, sir."

"And tell them all you know about the plane, the *Delos* and the survivors. Also our suspicions about the survivors. Saves the time when they get here."

"I'll do that. Speaking about the survivors, when I go ashore do you want me to take them along and dump them?"

"You are unwell, Number One?"

"I'm fine. Didn't for a moment think you'd want them out of your sight. And we couldn't very well abandon the two young ladies on that barren rock there."

"It's as well the islanders can't hear you. There's fourteen hundred people in the township of Thera and there's a fair amount of tourist accommodations. And speaking again of the survivors, not to mention our three other visitors, we'll have to find sleeping accommodations for them. The admiral can have the admiral's cabin—it'll be the first time an admiral has slept there. There are three empty cabins. You can have mine, I'll sleep here or in the chart room. The rest, well, you fix it."

"Five minutes," he said confidently.

He was back in forty-five.

"Took me a little longer than I thought. Ticklish problems."

"Who's got my cabin?"

"Irene. Eugenia has mine."

"It took you three-quarters of an hour to arrange that?"

"Decisions, decisions. Calls for a little delicacy and a modicum of finesse."

"My word, you do do yourselves well, Commander," Andropulous said. He sipped some claret. "Or is this a special treat for us?"

"Standard fare, I assure you." Andropulous, whom Grierson had reported as having a remarkable affinity for scotch, seemed relaxed to the point of garrulity. Talbot would have taken long odds that he was cold sober. He talked freely about quite a number of subjects, but had not once broached the question of being sent ashore. It was clear that he and Talbot had at least one thing in common—the wish that he remain aboard the *Ariadne*.

Jenkins came in and spoke softly to Van Gelder, who looked at Talbot.

"Call from the radio room. Shall I take it?" Talbot nodded. Van Gelder left and returned within half a minute.

"Call was delayed, sir. Difficulty in contacting us. They will be there in less than half an hour. I'd better go now."

"I'm expecting visitors later this evening," Talbot said. "I shall have to ask you not to come to the wardroom for some time after they come. Not for too long. Twenty minutes at the most."

"Visitors?" Andropulous said. "At this time of the evening? Who on earth are they?"

"I'm sorry, Mr. Andropulous. This is a naval vessel. There are certain things I can't discuss with civilians."

3

Vice Admiral Hawkins was the first up the gangway. He shook Talbot's hand warmly. The admiral didn't go in for saluting.

"Delighted to see you again, John. Or I would be if it weren't for the circumstances. And how are you, my boy?"

"Fine, sir. Again considering the circumstances."

"And the children? Little Fiona and Jimmy?"

"In the best, thank you, sir. You've come a long way in a short time."

"Needs must when the devil drives. And he's sitting on my tail right now." He turned to the two men who had followed him up the gangway. "Professor Benson. Dr. Wickram. Gentlemen, Commander Talbot, the captain of the *Ariadne*."

"If you will come with me, gentlemen. I'll have your gear taken to your quarters." Talbot led them to the wardroom and gestured them to their seats. "You want me to get my priorities right?"

"Certainly." Talbot pressed a bell and Jenkins came in. "A large gin and tonic for those two gentlemen," Hawkins said. "Lots of ice. They're Americans. Large scotch and water for me. Quarters, you said. What quarters?"

"You haven't been aboard since before commissioning but you won't have forgotten. For an admiral, an admiral's quarters. Never been used."

"How perfectly splendid. Honored, I'm sure. And for my two friends here?"

"A cabin apiece. Also never been used. I think they'll find them quite comfortable. I'd like to bring along some of my officers, sir."

"But of course. Whom did you have in mind?"

"Surgeon Commander Grierson."

"Know him," Hawkins said. "Very wise bird."

"Lieutenant Denholm. Our electronics wunderkind. I know you've met him, sir."

"That I have." He looked at his two friends, smiling broadly. "You'll have to mind your p's and q's here. Lieutenant Denholm is the heir to an earldom. The genuine article. Fearfully languid and aristocratic. Don't be deceived for an instant. Mind like a knife. As I told General Carson, he's so incredibly advanced in his electronic specialty that your high-tech whiz kids in Silicon Valley wouldn't even begin to understand what he's talking about."

"Then there's Lieutenant McCafferty, our senior engineer, and, of course, Lieutenant Commander Van Gelder, whom you've already met."

"For the first time. Favorably impressed. Very. Struck me as an able lad indeed."

"He's all that. More. If I were laid low tomorrow, you wouldn't have to worry. He could take over the *Ariadne* at any moment and you wouldn't notice the difference."

"From you, that's worth any half dozen testimonials. I'll bear it in mind."

Introductions completed, Hawkins looked at Talbot and his four officers and said, "The first question in your minds, of course, gentlemen, is why I have brought two civilians with me. First I will tell you who they are and then, when I have explained the purpose of our coming, you will understand why they are here. In passing, I might say how extraordinarily lucky I am to have them here with me. They seldom leave their home state of California; it just so happened that both were attending an international conference in Rome.

"Professor Alec Benson here." Benson was a large, calm man in his early sixties, gray of hair, cherubic and wearing a sports jacket, flannels and a polo jersey, all of varying shades of gray and all so lived in, comfortable and crumpled that he could well have inherited them from his grandfather. "The professor is the director of the seismological department of the California Institute of Technology in Pasadena. He's also a geologist and vulcanologist. Anything that makes the earth bang or shake or move is his field. Regarded by everybody in that line as the world's leading expert—he chaired, or was chairing until I so rudely interrupted him, an international conference in seismology in Rome. You all know, of course, what seismology is."

"A rough idea," Talbot said. "A kind of science, I think—'study' would be a better word for it—of the causes and effects of earthquakes."

"A kind of science?" Hawkins said. "I am distressed. It *is* a science."

"No offense meant, I'm sure, and none taken," Benson said equably. "The commander is perfectly correct. Far from being a science, we're still only dabbling on the periphery of the subject."

"Ah, well. Dr. Wickram is a physicist, as well known in his own field as Professor Benson is in his. He specializes in nuclear physics."

Talbot looked at Dr. Wickram, who, in startling contrast to Benson, was thin, dark and immaculately dressed in a blue suit, a white button-down collar and a black tie, the funeral hue of which went rather well with the habitual severity of his expression, and asked, "Does your interest in nuclear physics extend to nuclear weaponry, Dr. Wickram?"

"Well, yes, it does."

"You and the professor are to be congratulated. There should be some kind of civilian medal for this. Vice Admiral Hawkins, of course, is acting in the line of duty. I would have thought you two gentlemen would have stayed in Rome. I mean, isn't it safer there?"

Hawkins cleared his throat. "You wouldn't dream of stealing a superior officer's thunder, would you?"

"I wouldn't dream of it, sir."

"Well, to the point. Your two signals duly received. The first gave rise to some concern, the second was profoundly disturbing."

"The 'tick ... tick ... tick' bit, sir?"

"The 'tick ... tick ... tick' bit. Both signals were sent to the Pentagon, the second one also going to the White House. I should imagine that the word 'consternation' would suitably describe their reaction. Guessing, of course, but I think the speed of the reply to the second message showed how badly shaken they were. Normally, it can take forever—well, even months at times —to extract just a nugget of information from the Pentagon, but this time minutes only. When I read their reply, I could understand all too well." Hawkins paused, possibly for a suitably dramatic effect.

"So can I," Talbot said.

"What do you mean?"

"If I were the Pentagon or the White House I'd be upset, too, if a U.S. Air Force bomber or cargo plane, carrying a load of bombs, suddenly disappeared into the sea. Especially if the bombs—or missiles—that plane was carrying were of the nuclear variety. Even more especially if they were hydrogen bombs."

"Well, damn it, Talbot, you do deprive aging vice admirals of the simpler pleasures of life. There goes my thunder."

"It wasn't all that difficult, sir. We had already guessed it was a bomber. Civilian planes, with the exception of the Concorde, don't fly at the height at which we picked it up. We'd have had to be pretty stupid not to assume what we did. Bombers usually carry bombs. American reaction made it inevitable that it was an American plane. And you wouldn't have come down here in such a tearing hurry, and be accompanied by an expert in nuclear weaponry, unless the bombs were of a rather nasty variety. I can't imagine anything nastier than hydrogen bombs."

"Nor can anyone. When you put it the way you put it, I suppose that I should have guessed that you had guessed. Even the Pentagon don't know or won't divulge what type of plane it was. They suggest an advanced design of the C-141 Starlifter cargo plane. It was refueled in the Azores and heading for Greece. From your first message we gathered you saw the plane crash into the sea but couldn't identify it. Why not?"

"Number One, show the admiral why not."

Van Gelder produced a sheaf of photographs and handed them to Hawkins, who flipped through them quickly and then, more slowly, a second time. He sighed and looked up.

"Intriguing, I suppose, if you're a connoisseur

of the pattern effects of smoke and flame. I'm not. All I can make out is what I take to be the outer port engine and that's no help at all. And it gives no indication as to the source or cause of the fire."

"I think Van Gelder would disagree with you, sir," Talbot said. "He's of the opinion that the fire originated in the nose cone and was caused by an internal explosion. I agree with him. It certainly wasn't brought down by ship-based antiaircraft fire. We would have known. The only alternative is a heat-seeking missile. Two objections to that. Such a missile would have targeted on the engines, not the fuselage, and, more importantly, there are no vessels in the area. Our radar would have picked them up. As a corollary to that, the missile didn't come from an aircraft, either. The admiral will not need reminding that the radar aboard the *Ariadne* is as advanced as any in the world."

"That may no longer be true, sir." Denholm's tone was deferential but not hesitant. "And if that's true, then we can't discount missiles just like that. This is not a dissenting opinion, I'm just exploring another possibility."

"Explore away, Lieutenant," Hawkins said.

"I'm not sure I'm all that good as a beacon, sir. I do know that I don't go along with the belief that the Soviets always trail the West in technological advancement. Whether this belief is carefully and officially nurtured, I do not know. I admit that the Soviets spend a certain amount of time and trouble in extracting military secrets from the West. I say 'certain' because they don't have to try all that hard; there appears to be a steady supply of scientists, both American and British, who, along with associates not necessarily involved in direct research at all, are perfectly willing to sell the Soviets anything they want—provided, that is, the price is right. I believe this to be true in the case of computers, where they do lag behind the West; I do not believe it in the case or radar.

"In this field, Plessey, of Britain, probably leads the West. They have developed a revolutionary new radar system, the Type 966, which is fitted, or about to be fitted, to Invincible-class aircraft carriers, the Type 42 Sheffield-class destroyers and the new Type 23 Norfolk-class frigates. This new radar is designed not only to detect and track aircraft and sea-skimming missiles, but they also—"

Hawkins cleared his throat. "Sorry to interrupt, Denholm. You may know this but surely it comes under the heading of classified information?"

"If it did, I wouldn't talk about it even in this company. It's in the public domain. As I was about to say, it's also able to control Sea Dart and Seawolf missiles in flight and home them in on their targets with great accuracy. I also understand they're virtually immune to jamming and radar decoys. If Plessey has done this the Soviets may well have also. They're not much given to advertising such things. But I believe they have the know-how."

Hawkins said, "And you also believe, in this case, that a missile was the culprit?"

"Not at all, sir. I'm only suggesting a possibility. The captain and Lieutenant Commander Van Gelder may well be right. Trouble is, I know nothing about explosives. Maybe there are missiles with such a limited charge that they cause only limited damage. I would have thought that a standard missile would have ensured that a plane it brought down would have struck the sea, not with its fuselage relatively intact, but in a thousand pieces. Again, I simply don't know. I just wonder what the security was like at the base from which that plane took off in the States."

"Security? In the case of a supersensitive plane such as this? Total."

"Does the admiral really believe there is such a thing as total security?" Hawkins just sipped his scotch in silence. "There were four major air disasters last year, all four planes involved having taken off from airports which were regarded as having maximum security. In all four cases terrorists found the most stringent airports checks childishly easy to circumvent."

"Those were civilian airports. This would be a top-secret U.S. Air Force base, manned exclusively by U.S. Air Force personnel, specially chosen for their position, rigidly screened, backgrounds exhaustively researched and all subjected to lie-detector tests."

"With respect to the vice admiral, and our American friends, lie-detector tests—more accurately, polygraph tests—are rubbish. Any moderately intelligent person can be trained to beat the polygraph test, which, after all, depends on crudely primitive measurements of pulse rates, blood pressure and perspiration. You can be trained to give right answers, wrong answers or merely confusing ones and the scrutineer can't tell the difference."

"Doesn't measure up to your idea of electronics, eh?"

"Nothing to do with electronics, sir. Polygraphs belong to the horse-and-buggy era. You've just used the word 'supersensitive,' sir. The *Ariadne,* if I may put it that way, is a hotbed of supersensitivity. How many members of this crew have ever been subjected to a polygraph test? None."

Hawkins considered his glass for a few moments, then looked up at Talbot. "Should the need arise, Captain, how long would it take you to contact the Pentagon?"

"Immediately. Well, half a minute. Now?"

"No. Wait. Have to think about it. Trouble is, even the Pentagon is having difficulty in extracting information from this Air Force base, which is, I believe, somewhere in Georgia. The Pentagon's own fault, really, although you can't expect them to admit it. They've so inculcated this passion for absolute secrecy into the senior officers of all four services that no one is prepared to reveal anything without the permission of the commanding officer of the Air Force base or ship or whatever. In this particular case, the commanding officer, who, to the Pentagon's distress, would appear to have a human side to his nature, has elected to take twenty-four hours off. No one seems to know where he is."

Van Gelder said, "Makes it a bit awkward, sir, doesn't it, if war breaks out in the next half hour?"

"No. Base remains in full operational readiness. But there's still no relaxation of the ironbound rules concerning the release of classified information."

Talbot said, "You wouldn't be sitting here unless they'd released *some* information."

"Naturally not. The news they've released is vague and incomplete but all very, very bad. One report says there were twelve nuclear weapons aboard, another fifteen. Whether they were missiles or bombs was not disclosed; what was disclosed was that they are hydrogen devices, each one in the monster megaton range, twelve to fifteen megatons. The plane was also understood to be carrying two of the more conventional atom bombs."

"I think I'll break a self-imposed regulation and have a scotch myself," Talbot said. A half minute passed in silence, then he said quietly, "This is worse than I ever dreamed."

"Dream?" Grierson said. "Nightmare."

"Dream or nightmare, it won't matter to us," Lieutenant Denholm said. "Not when we're drifting through the stratosphere in vaporized orbit."

"A hydrogen bomb, Dr. Wickram," Talbot said. "Let's call it that. Is there any way it can spontaneously detonate?"

"In itself, impossible. The President of the United States has to press one button, the man on the spot another; the radio frequencies are so wildly different that the chances of anyone happening on the right combination are billions to one."

"Is there a chance—say, a billion to one—that the Soviets might have this combination?"

"None."

"You say it's impossible to detonate in itself. Is there any other way, some external means, whereby it could be detonated?"

"I don't know."

"Does that mean you're not saying or that you're not sure? I don't think, Dr. Wickram, that this is the time to dwell on such verbal niceties."

"I'm not sure. If there was a sufficiently powerful explosion close by, it might go up by sympathetic detonation. We simply don't know."

"The possibility has never been explored? I mean, no experiments?"

"I should hope not," Lieutenant Denholm said. "If such an experiment were successful, I wouldn't care to be within thirty or forty miles at the time."

"That is one point." For the first time, Dr. Wickram attempted a smile, but it was a pretty wintry one. "In the second place, quite frankly, we have never envisaged a situation where such a possibility might arise. We could, I suppose, have carried out such an experiment without the drastic consequences the lieutenant has suggested. We could detonate a very small atom bomb in the vicinity of another. Even a charge of conventional explosive in the vicinity of a small atom bomb would suffice. If the small atom bomb went up, then so would the hydrogen bomb. Everybody knows that it's the fissioning of an atom bomb that triggers off the fusion of a hydrogen bomb."

Talbot said, "Is there any timing device, specifically a delayed one, fitted in a hydrogen bomb?"

"None." The flat finality in the voice left no room for argument.

"According to Vice Admiral Hawkins, there may be a couple of conventional atom bombs aboard the sunken plane. Could they be fitted with timing devices?"

"Again, I don't know. Not my field. But I see no reason why they couldn't be."

"For what purpose?"

"Search me. Realms of speculation, Captain, where your guess is as good as mine. The only thing that occurs to me is a mine, a marine mine.

Neatly dispose of any passing aircraft carrier, I should think."

"That's thinking small," Van Gelder said. "A hydrogen mine would neatly dispose of any passing battle fleet."

"Whose passing fleet? One of ours? In wartime as in peacetime, the seas are open to all."

"Not in the Black Sea. Not in wartime. But a bit farfetched. How would this mine be activated?"

"My continued ignorance must be a great disappointment. I know nothing about mines."

"Well, time was when mines were either magnetic or acoustic. Degaussing has made magnetic mines passé. So, acoustic. Triggered by a passing ship's engines. Interesting, isn't it? I mean, we've passed over it several times since we first heard the ticking and we've triggered nothing. So far. So maybe that ticking doesn't mean that the mine is set to go off anytime. Maybe it's not activated— by which I mean ready to go off when a vessel passes over it—until the ticking stops. Trouble is, we've no idea what started the ticking in the first place. I can't see any way it could have been deliberate. Must have been caused by the explosion that brought down the plane or by the impact of striking the water."

"You're a source of great comfort, Van Gelder," Hawkins said heavily.

"I admit, sir, that the alternatives aren't all that attractive. My own conclusions, which in this care are probably completely worthless, are that this ticking represents a period of grace—I mean that it cannot explode as long as the ticking lasts—and that it's not designed to explode when the ticking stops but is then activated and ready to explode when triggered by passing engines. A guess, sir, but not necessarily a wild one. I'm going on the assumption that this mine could well be dropped by a surface vessel as well as a plane. In that case, the ship would want to be a large number of miles away before the mine was activated. So it would start the timing mechanism running at the moment it dropped it over the side. I am sure, sir, that the Pentagon could provide some illumination on this subject."

"I'm sure they could," Hawkins said. "And your conclusions are far from worthless; they make a good deal of sense to me. Well, Captain, what do you propose to do about all this?"

"I rather thought, sir, that your purpose in coming down here was to tell *me* what to do."

"Not at all. I just came to bring myself up to date on the situation and to garner some information in return for some I give you."

"Does this mean, Admiral—I say this carefully, you understand—that I have a hand in making the decisions?"

"You don't have a hand. You damn well make them. I'll endorse them."

"Thank you. Then my first decision—or, if you like, a suggestion respectfully made—is that you and your two friends depart for Rome immediately. It's not going to help anyone, and will be a considerable loss to the scientific and naval communities, if you three gentlemen elect for self-immolation. Besides, by asking me to make the decisions, you have implied that there's nothing you can do here that my crew and I can't. Lieutenant Commander Van Gelder is at your immediate service."

"The lieutenant commander will have to wait. For me, at least. Your logic is sound but I'm not feeling very logical at the moment. But I do agree as far as my two friends are concerned. They could be back at their international conference in Rome tomorrow, without anyone's having noticed their absence. We have no right to put the lives of civilians, not to mention two such eminent civilians, at risk."

"You've just put your finger on it, Admiral." Benson puffed comfortably on a sadly blackened pipe. "Eminent or not, we are civilians. Civilians don't take orders from the military. I prefer the Aegean to Rome."

"Agreed," Wickram said.

"You don't seem to have any more clout with your two friends than I have with the three of you." Talbot produced two slips of paper from his inner pocket. "I suggest you sign those, sir."

Hawkins took them, looked thoughtfully at Talbot, scanned the two sheets, then read from one of them.

"'Request urgent immediate dispatch of nearest salvage or diving vessel to 36.21N, 25.22E

due south Cape Akrotiri, Thera Island, to recover one sunken plane, one sunken yacht. Further request immediate dispatch by plane to
Thera Island two deep-sea divers with diving
equipment for four, repeat four. Priority one
double A. Signed Vice Admiral Hawkins,'" Hawkins looked at Benson and Wickram. "This message is directed to Rear Admiral Blyth, HMS
Apollo. Read Admiral Blyth is the operational
commander of the European section of NATO
sea forces in the eastern Mediterranean. Priority
one double A means drop everything else, this
has absolute priority. Admiral Hawkins is, I take
it, my good self. Why, Captain, the request for
four diving suits?"

"Van Gelder and I are trained divers, sir. Ex-
sub-mariners."

"I see. Second signal directed to Defense
Minister, Athens. 'Urgent contact Air Control
Athens airport for information re aircraft,
thought American, that crashed 1415 today
south of Thera Island. Did it ask permission for
flight path to, and landing in, Athens or other
Greek airfield? Further request you enlist immediate aid of police and intelligence re anything
known about one Spyros Andropulous, owner of
yacht *Delos*.' This message is also, I'm flattered
to observe, signed by me. Well, well, well, Captain, I nearly did you a great injustice a minute
or two ago; I thought you had not perhaps addressed yourself to the problem on hand. But

you have, and in some style and quite some time before I arrived. Two questions."

"The aircraft and Andropulous?" Hawkins nodded. "At fifty-three thousand feet, the pilot didn't have to bother to notify anyone about his presence. He knew he was alone in the sky. But once he started descending, it was a different matter entirely. He wouldn't be too keen on bumping into anyone, especially not with the cargo he had on board. And, of course, he would require permission to land."

"But why Greece?"

"Because the flight path he was following when we first located him would have taken him to Ankara in Turkey, or some place pretty close by. Now, even though Turkey is—nominally at least—a member of NATO, I'm sure the Americans have no air bases at, or near, Ankara. I don't even know if they have any air bases at all in Turkey. I'm certain they have no missile-launching bases. In Greece, the Americans have both. So, Greece. As for Andropulous, several of my officers and I think he's a leery customer and a suspicious one. Not one thing that could be proved in a court of law, of course. We suspect that he may know something about the downing of this plane that we don't *know* he knows, if you follow me. He says the *Delos* was sunk as the result of an explosion. But it's the old question of did he fall or was he pushed? In other words, was the explosion accidental or deliberate? If we could hoist the *Delos* to the surface we might well find out."

"We might well indeed. Still, first things first." Hawkins looked briefly at the signals again. "These seem to fit the task admirably. I'll gladly sign." Hawkins produced a pen, signed and handed the papers to Talbot. "As you had all this figured out quite some time ago, I suspect before I left Rome, why didn't you send those signals yourself?"

"Lowly commanders don't give instructions to Rear Admiral Blyth. I haven't the authority. You have. That's why I asked you to join us as soon as was possible. Thanks for the signing, sir. That was the easy part. Now comes the difficult part."

"Difficult part?" Hawkins said warily. "What difficult part?"

"Have we the moral right to ask the crew of the salvage vessel or lifting vessel, not to mention the divers, to join us, in Lieutenant Denholm's elegant phrase, in drifting through the stratosphere in vaporized orbit?"

"Ah. Yes. A point, of course. What do *you* think?"

"Again, not a decision for lowly commanders. Admirals only."

"If things go wrong, you'll have nothing on your conscience and everything in the world to reproach me with."

"If anything goes wrong, sir, I don't think we'll

be having too much to say to each other when we're in vaporized orbit."

"True. Mine was an unworthy remark. No one likes to bear the responsibility for such decisions. Send the signals."

"Very good, sir. Lieutenant Denholm, ask Myers to come here."

Hawkins said, "I understand—I'm not making comparisons—that the President of the United States was faced with a problem similar to the one you've just confronted me with. He asked the Chairman of the Joint Chiefs of Staff if he should pull out the *Ariadne*, which they knew, of course, was sitting over the crashed plane. The Chairman said, quite rightly, that that wasn't his responsibility, the old and honored American tradition of passing the buck. The President decided that the *Ariadne* should stay."

"Well, I could be bitter about that and say that's very noble and gallant of the President, especially as there's no chance of his being blown out of his seat in the Oval Office when this little lot goes up, but I won't. It's not a decision I would care to have to make. I assume he gave a reason for his decision?"

"Yes. The greatest good of the greatest number."

Myers came in. Talbot handed him the two messages.

"Get these off at once. Code B in both cases. To both messages add 'Immediate, repeat immediate, confirmation is requested.'" Myers left and

Talbot said, "It is my understanding, Admiral, that in your capacity as officer commanding the naval forces in the eastern Mediterranean you have the power to overrule the President's instructions."

"Yes."

"Have you done so?"

"No. You will ask why. Same reason as the President. The greatest good of the greatest number. Why the questioning, Captain? You wouldn't leave here even if I gave a direct order."

"I'm just a bit puzzled about the reason given —the greatest good of the greatest number. Bringing a rescue vessel, which admittedly is my idea, will only increase the greatest danger to a greater number."

"I don't think you quite appreciate just how great the greatest number is in this case. I think Professor Benson here can enlighten you. Enlighten all of us, for I'm rather vague about it. That's why Professor Benson is here."

"The good professor is not at his best," Benson said. "He's hungry."

"Most remiss of us," Talbot said. "Of course, you haven't eaten. Dinner, say, in twenty minutes?"

"I'd settle for a sandwich." Talbot looked at Hawkins and Wickram, both of whom nodded. He pressed a bell.

"I'm a bit vague about it myself," Benson said. "Certain facts are beyond dispute. What we're sitting on top of at this moment is one of them. According to which estimate of the Pentagon's you choose to believe, there's something like a total of between 144 and 225 megatons of high explosive lying down there. Not that the difference between the lowest and the highest estimate is of any significance. The explosion of a pound of high explosive in this wardroom would kill us all. What we are talking about is the explosive power of, let me see, yes, four and a half billion pounds. The human mind cannot comprehend, differences in estimates become irrelevant. All we can say with certainty is that it would be the biggest manmade explosion in history, which doesn't sound so bad when you say it as quickly as I'm saying it now.

"The results of such an explosion are quite unknown but stupefyingly horrendous however optimistic your guess might be. It might fracture the earth's crust, with cataclysmic results. It might destroy part of the ozone layer, which would permit the sun's ultraviolet radiation to either tan us or fry us, depending upon how large a hole had been blasted in the stratosphere. It might equally well cause the onset of a nuclear winter, which is so popular a topic among both scientists and laymen these days. And lastly, but by no means least, are the tsunami effects, vast tidal waves usually generated by undersea earthquakes. Those tsunamis have been responsible for the deaths of tens of thousands of people at a time when they struck low-lying coastal areas."

Benson reached out a grateful hand for a glass that Jenkins had brought. Talbot said, "If you're trying to be encouraging, Professor, you're not doing too well at it."

"Ah, better, much better." Benson lowered his glass and sighed. "I needed that. There are times when I'm quite capable of terrifying even myself. Encouraging? That's only the half of it. Santorini's the other half. In fact, Santorini is the major part of it. Gifted though mankind is at creating sheer wanton destruction, nature has him whacked every time."

"Santorini?" Wickram said. "Who or what is Santorini?"

"Ignorance, George, ignorance. You and your fellow physicists should look out from your ivory towers from time to time. Santorini is less than a couple of miles from where you're sitting. Had that name for many centuries. Today it's officially known, as it was five thousand years ago at the height of its civilization, as Thera Island.

"The island, by whatever name, has had a very turbulent seismic and volcanic history. Don't worry, George, I'm not about to sally forth on my old hobbyhorse, not for long anyway, just long enough to try to explain what the greatest number means in the term 'the greatest good of the greatest number.'

"It is commonly enough imagined that earthquakes and volcanic eruptions are two faces of the same coin. This is not necessarily so. The venerable Oxford English Dictionary states that an earthquake is specifically a convulsion of the earth's surface caused by volcanic forces. The dictionary is specifically wrong: it should have used the word 'rarely' instead. Earthquakes, especially the big ones, are caused when two tectonic plates—segments of the earth's crust that float freely on the molten magma beneath—come into contact with one another and one plate bangs into the other or rubs alongside it or dives under it. The only two recorded and monitored giant earthquakes in history were of this type—in Ecuador in 1906 and Japan in 1933. Similarly, but on a lesser scale—although still very big—the California earthquakes at San Francisco and the Owens Valley were due to crustal movement and not to volcanoes.

"It is true that practically all the world's five to six hundred active volcanoes—someone may have bothered to count them; I haven't—are located along convergent plate boundaries. It is equally true that they are rarely associated with earthquakes. There have been three large volcanic eruptions along such boundaries in very recent years: Mount St. Helens in the state of Washington, El Chichón in Mexico and one just northwest of Bogotá in Columbia. The last one —it happened only last year—was particularly nasty. A seventeen-thousand-foot volcano called Nevada del Ruiz, which seems to have been slumbering off and on for the past four hundred years, erupted and melted the snow and ice which covered most of its upper reaches, giving rise to an estimated seventy-five-million-cubic-yard mudslide. The town of Armero stood in its way. Twenty-five thousand people died there. The point is that none of those was accompanied by an earthquake. Even volcanoes in areas where there are no established tectonic frontiers are guiltless in this respect. Vesuvius—despite the fact that it buried Pompeii and Herculaneum—Stromboli, Mount Etna and the twin volcanoes of the island of Hawaii have not produced, and do not produce, earthquakes.

"But the really bad apples in the seismic barrel, and a very sinister lot those are, too, are the so-called thermal hot spots, plumes or upswellings of molten lava that reach up to or through the earth's crust, giving rise to volcanoes or earthquakes or both. We talk a lot about those thermal plumes but we really don't know much about them. We don't know whether they're localized or whether they spread out and lubricate the movements of the tectonic plates. What we do know is that they can have extremely unpleasant effects. One of those was responsible for the biggest earthquake of this century."

"You have me confused, Professor," Hawkins said. "You've just mentioned the really big ones, the ones in Japan and Ecuador. But those were monitored and recorded. This one wasn't?"

"Certainly it was. But countries like Russia and China are rather coy about releasing such details. They have the weird notion that natural disasters reflect upon their political systems."

"Is it in order to ask how you know?"

"Of course. Governments may elect not to talk to governments but we scientists are an incurably gabby lot. This quake happened at the town of Tangshan in northeastern China and is the only one ever known to have occurred in a really densely populated area, in this case involving the major cities of Peking and Tientsin. The primary cause was undobutedly a thermal plume. There are no known tectonic-plate boundaries in the area but a very ancient boundary may be lurking there. The date was July 27, 1976."

"Yesterday," Hawkins said. "Just yesterday. Casualties?"

"Two-thirds of a million dead, three-quarters of a million injured. Give or take a hundred thousand in each case. If that sounds flippant or heartless, it's not meant to be. After a certain arbitrary figure—a hundred thousand, ten thousand, even a thousand, it all depends upon how much your heart and mind can take—any increase in numbers becomes meaningless. And there's also the factor, of course, that we're referring to faceless unknowns in a far-off land."

"I suppose," Hawkins said, "that that would be what one might call the granddaddy of them all?"

"In terms of lives lost, it probably is. We can't be sure. What we can be sure of is that Tangshan rates as no more than third in the cataclysmic league. Just over a century ago the island of Krakatoa in Indonesia blew itself out of existence. That was quite a bang, literally—the sound of the explosion was heard thousands of miles away. So much volcanic material was blasted into the stratosphere that the world was still being treated to a series of spectacular sunsets more than three years afterward. No one knows the height of the tsunami caused by this eruption. What we do know is that much of the three great islands bordering the Java Sea—Sumatra, Java and Borneo—and nearly all of the smaller islands inside the sea itself lie below an altitude of two hundred feet. No tally of the dead has ever been made. It is better, perhaps, that we don't know."

"And perhaps it's also better that we don't know what you're going to say next," Talbot said. "I don't much care for the road you're leading us along."

"I don't much care for it myself." Benson sighed and sipped some more gin. "Anyone ever heard of the word *kalliste*?"

"Certainly," Denholm said. "Means most beautiful. Very ancient. Goes back to Homeric times."

"My goodness." Benson peered at him through his pipe smoke. "I thought you were the electronics officer?"

"Lieutenant Denholm is primarily a classicist," Talbot said. "Electronics is one of his hobbies."

"Ah!" Benson gestured with his thumb. "Kalliste was the name given to this little lady before it became either Thera or Santorini, and a more singularly inappropriate name I cannot imagine. It was this beautiful lady that blew her top in 1450 B.C. with four times the explosively destructive power of Krakatoa. What had been the cone of a volcano became a circular depression—we call it a caldera—some thirty square miles in area, into which the sea poured. Stirring times, gentlemen, stirring times.

"Unfortunately those stirring times are still with us. Santorini has had, and continues to have, a very turbulent seismic history. Incidentally, mythology has it that there was an even bigger eruption about twenty-five thousand years ago. However, it hasn't done too badly since 1450 B.C. In 236 B.C. another eruption separated Therasia from northwestern Thera. Forty years later the islet of old Jaimeni appeared. There have been bangs and explosions, the appearances and disappearances of islands and volcanoes ever since. In the late sixteenth century the south coast of Thera, together with the port of Eleusis, vanished under the sea and stayed there. Even as late as 1956 a considerable earthquake destroyed half the buildings on the west coast of the island. Santorini, one fears, rests on very shaky foundations."

Talbot said, "What happened in 1450 B.C.?"

"Regrettably, our ancestors of some thirty-five centuries back don't seem to have given too much thought to posterity, by which I mean they left no records to satisfy their descendants' intellectual curiosity. One can hardly blame them; they had too many urgent and pressing matters on hand at the time to worry about such things. According to one account, the explosion caused a tidal wave a hundred sixty-five feet high. I don't know who worked this out. I don't believe it. It is true that water levels on the Alaskan coast, caused by tsunamis, earthquake-related tidal waves, have risen over three hundred feet, but this only happens when the seabed shallows close inshore; in the deep sea, although the tsunamis can travel tremendously fast, two, perhaps three hundred miles an hour, it's rarely more than a ripple on the surface of the water.

"The experts are deeply divided as to what happened. 'Loggerheads' would be too mild a term. It's an archeological minefield. The explosion *may* have destroyed the Cyclades. It *may* have wiped out the Minoan civilization in Crete. It *may* have swamped the Aegean isles and the coastal lowlands of Greece and Turkey. It may have inundated Lower Egypt, flooded the Nile and swept back the Red Sea waters to permit the escape of the Canaanites fleeing from the Pharoah. That's one view. In 1950 a scientist by the name of Immanuel Velikovsky caused a considerable furor in the historical, religious and astronomical worlds by stating unequivocally that the flooding was caused by Venus, which had been wrenched free from Jupiter and made an uncomfortably close encounter with Earth. A very scholarly and erudite work, widely acclaimed at the time but since much maligned. Professional jealousy? Upsetting the scientific applecart? A charlatan? Unlikely—the man was a friend and colleague of Albert Einstein. Then, of course, there was Edmund Halley, of comet fame—he was equally certain that the flooding had been caused by a passing comet.

"There's no doubt there was a huge natural disaster all those millennia ago. As to its cause, take your pick—your guess is as good as mine. Reverting to the situation we find ourselves in at this moment, there are four facts that can be regarded as certainties or near certainties. First, Santorini is about as stable as the proverbial blancmange. Second, it's sitting on top of a thermal plume. Third, the chances are high that it is sitting atop an ancient tectonic boundary that runs east-west under the Mediterranean— this is where the African and Eurasian plates are in contention. Fourth, and indisputably, *we* are sitting atop the equivalent of roughly two hundred million tons of TNT. If that goes up, I would say it is highly probable—in fact I think I should use the word 'inevitable'—that both the thermal plume and the temporarily quiescent earthquake zone along the tectonic fault would be reactivated. I leave the rest to your imagination." Benson drained his glass and looked around hopefully. Talbot pressed a bell.

Hawkins said, "I don't have that kind of imagination."

"None of us has. Fortunately. We're talking

about the combined and simultaneous effect of a massive thermonuclear detonation, a volcanic eruption and an earthquake. This lies outside the experience of mankind, so we can't visualize those things except to guess, and it's a safe guess, that the reality will be worse than any nightmare. The only consolation, of course, is that we wouldn't be around to experience anything, nightmare or reality.

"The extent of potential annihilation is beyond belief. By 'annihilation' I mean the total extinction of life, except possibly some subterranean or aquatic forms. What lava, volcanic cinders, dust and ashes don't get, the blast, air percussion waves, fire and tsunami will. If there are any survivors within an area of thousands of square miles the massive radioactive fallout will attend to them. It hardly seems necessary to talk about such things as nuclear winters and being fried by ultraviolet radiation.

"So you can see, Commander Talbot, what we mean when we talk about the greatest good of the greatest number. What does it matter if we have two ships or ten out here, two hundred men or two thousand? Every extra man, every extra ship may, just may, be of a tiny percentage more help in neutralizing this damn thing on the sea floor. What's even two thousand compared to the unimaginable numbers who might perish if that device does detonate sooner or later—almost certainly sooner—if we don't do something about it?"

"You put things very nicely, Professor, and you make things very clear. Not that the *Ariadne* had any intention of going anywhere, but it's nice to have a solid reason to stay put." He thought briefly. "Solves one little problem anyway. I have six survivors from the yacht *Delos* aboard and had thought to put three of the innocent parties among them ashore, but that seems a little pointless now."

"Alas, yes. Whether they are aboard here or on Santorini it will be all one to them when they join us in what Lieutenant Denholm is pleased to call vaporized orbit."

Talbot lifted a phone, asked for a number, listened briefly and hung up.

"The sonar room. Still tick... tick... tick."

"Ah," Benson said. "Tick... tick.... tick."

4

"You had an enjoyable tête-a-tête with Mr. Andropulous, sir?" Vice Admiral Hawkins, together with his two scientist friends, had just come to the bridge in response to Talbot's invitation that they join him.

"Enjoyable? Ha! Thank you, incidentally, for rescuing us. Enjoyable? Depends what you mean, John."

"I mean, were you suitably impressed?"

"I was suitably unimpressed. Interested, mind you, but deeply unimpressed. Man's character, I mean, not his quite extraordinary affinity for strong spirits. He comes across as whiter than the driven snow. A man of such transparent honesty has to have something to hide."

"And he got his slurring wrong, too," Benson said.

"Slurring, sir?"

"Just that, Commander. Thickened his voice in the wrong places in trying to convince us that he was under the influence. Maybe he could have gotten away with it in his native Greek but not in English. Cold sober, I believe. And clever. Anyway, he's clever enough to hoodwink those two charming young ladies he has with him. I *think* they're being hoodwinked."

"And his bosom friend, Alexander," Hawkins said. "He's not so clever. He comes over as what he might well be—a paid-up member, if not a capo, in the Mafia. He was quite unmoved when I sympathized with them about the loss of the three members of their crew. Andropulous said he was desolated by the deaths of his treasured friends. Van Gelder had already told us that. Maybe he was overcome by grief, maybe not. In view of the fact that, like you, I regard him as a fluent liar and consummate actor, I think not. Maybe he is conscience-stricken at having arranged their deaths. Again, I think not. I don't mean he couldn't have been responsible for their deaths, I just mean that I don't think he's on speaking terms with is conscience. Only information I gathered from him his that he left his yacht because he thought his spare fuel tank was going to blow up. A man of mystery, your newfound friend."

"He's all that. Very mysterious. He's a multimillionaire. Maybe a multi-multimillionaire. Not in the usual Greek line of tankers—bottom's fallen out of that market anyway. He's an international businessman with contacts in many countries."

Hawkins said, "Van Gelder told me nothing of this."

"Of course he didn't. He didn't know. Your name attached to a message, Admiral, is a guarantee of remarkably quick service. Reply to our query to the Greek Defense Ministry received twenty-five minutes ago."

"A businessman. What kind of business?"

"They didn't say. I knew that would be your question, so I immediately radioed a request for that information."

"Signed by me, of course."

"Naturally, sir. Had it been a different matter I would of course have asked your permission. But this was the same matter. The reply came in a few minutes ago listing ten different countries with which he does business."

"Again, what kind of business?"

"Again, they didn't say."

"Extraordinarily odd. What do you make of it?"

"The Foreign Minister must have authorized this reply. Maybe censored it a little. He is, of course, a member of the government. I would assume that the mysterious Mr. Andropulous has friends in the government."

"The mysterious Mr. Andropulous gets more mysterious by the moment."

"Maybe, sir. Maybe not—not when you consider the list of ten foreign trading partners he has. Four of them are in cities that you might regard as being of particular interest—Tripoli, Beirut, Damascus and Baghdad."

"Indeed." Hawkins thought briefly. "Gunrunning?"

"But of course, sir. Nothing illegal about being gunrunners—Britain and America are overrun with them. But all governments are holier-than-thou in this respect and never publicly associate themselves with them. Never do to be classified as a merchant of death. Could well explain why the Greek government is being so cagey."

"Indeed, it could."

"One thing strikes me as odd. Why is Tehran missing from the list?"

"True, true. The Iranians—with the possible exception of the Afghans—are more desperate for arms than any other place around. But gunrunners don't specialize in blowing up planes in flight."

"I don't know what we're talking about, sir. The Hampton Court maze has nothing on this lot. I have the feeling that it's going to take us quite some time to figure this out. Fortunately, we have more immediate problems to occupy our minds."

"Fortunately?" Hawkins lifted his eyes heavenward. "Did you say fortunately?"

"Yes, sir. Vincent?" Talbot turned to Van Gelder. "I should think Jenkins knows the requirements of the vice admiral and his two friends by this time."

"You are not joining us?" Benson said.

"Better not. We expect to be quite busy later on tonight." He turned to Van Gelder again. "And give orders for our six shipwrecked mariners to return to their cabins. They are to remain there until further orders. Post guards to see that those instructions are obeyed."

"I think I'd better go and do this myself, sir."

"Fine. I'm all out of tact at the moment."

Hawkins said, "Do you think they'll take kindly to this—ah—incarceration?"

"Incarceration? Let's call it protective custody. Fact is, I don't want them to see what's going on in the next few hours. I'll explain why in a moment."

"The Ministry of Defense had another item of information for us. About the bomber. It *had* been in touch with Air Control in Athens and had been instructed to alter course over the island of Amorgos—that's about forty miles northeast of here—and proceed in a roughly north-northwest course. Two fighter planes—U.S. Air Force F-15s—went up to meet it and escort it in."

"Did you see any such planes in the vicinity?"

"No, sir. Wouldn't have expected to. Rendezvous point was to be over the island of Euboea. The destination was not Athens but Thessalonica. I assume the Americans have a missile base in that area. I wouldn't know."

"Admiral Blyth on the *Apollo* has also come through. We've had luck here—two pieces of luck. A recovery ship en route to Piraeus has been diverted to Santorini. Diving crews, recovery gear, the lot. You'll know it sir. The *Kilcharran*."

"I know it. Auxiliary Fleet vessel. Nominally under my command. I say 'nominally' because I also have the misfortune to know its captain. Lad called Montgomery. A very crusty Irishman with a low opinion of Royal Navy regulations. Not that that matters. He's brilliant at his job. Couldn't ask to have a better man around. Your other item of good news?"

"There's a plane en route to Santorini at this moment with a couple of divers and diving equipment for four aboard. Very experienced men, I'm told, a chief petty officer and a petty officer. I've sent Sublieutenant Cousteau ashore to pick them up. They should be here in half an hour or so."

"Excellent, excellent. And when do you expect the *Kilcharran*?"

"About five in the morning, sir."

"Things are looking up. You have something in mind?"

"Yes, sir. It will also answer your two questions —why Van Gelder and I are on the wagon and why the six survivors have been, well, locked up out of harm's way. When Cousteau comes back with the divers and equipment, Van Gelder and I are going down with them to have a look at this plane. I'm pretty sure we won't be able to accomplish much. But we'll be able to assess the extent of the damage to the plane, with luck locate this ticking monster and with even greater luck manage to free it. I know in advance that we're not going to have that kind of luck but it's worth a try. You'd be the first to agree, sir, that in the circumstances, *anything* is worth a try."

"Yes, yes, but you'll excuse me if I frown a bit. You and Van Gelder are the two most important people on this ship."

"No, we're not. If anything should happen to us personally, and I don't see what can happen, you are, in your spare time, so to speak, accustomed to commanding a battle fleet. I can hardly see that a mere frigate is going to inconvenience you to all that extent. And if anything should happen on a catastrophic scale, nobody's going to be worrying too much about anything."

Wickram said, "You are cold-blooded, Commander."

Hawkins sighed. "Not cold blood, Dr. Wickram. Cold logic, I'm afraid. And when and if you come back up, what then?"

"Then we're off to have a look at the *Delos*. Should be very interesting. Andropulous may have made a mistake, Admiral, in telling you that he was scared that his spare fuel tank might blow up. But then, he could have had no idea that we were going to have a look at the *Delos*. That's why he's locked up. I don't want him to know we've got divers aboard and I especially don't want him to see me taking off with divers in the general direction of the *Delos*. If we find that there *was* no spare tank, we shall have to keep an even closer eye on him—and, for good measure, on his dear friend Alexander and his captain, Aristotle. I can't

believe that that young seaman, Achmed or whatever his name is, or either of the two girls can
have anything to do with this. I think they're
along for the purpose of camouflage, respectabil-
ity, if you will. In any event, we should be back
long before the *Kilcharran* arrives." He turned to
look at Denholm, who had just arrived on the
bridge. "Well, Jimmy, what drags you away from
the fleshpots?"

"If I may say so with some dignity, sir, I'm trying to set them an example. I've just had a
thought, sir. If you will excuse me, Admiral?"

"I think that any thought you might have could
be well worth listening to, young man. Not Greek
literature, this time, I'll be bound. This—ah—
hobby of yours. Electronics, is it not?"

"Well, yes it is, sir." Denholm seemed faintly
surprised. He looked at Talbot. "That atom bomb
down there, the one that goes tick…tick…tick.
The intention, or the hope anyway, is to detach it
from the other explosives?"

"If it can be done."

"And then, sir?"

"One thing at a time, Jimmy. That's as far as
my thinking has got so far."

"Would we try to deactivate it?" Denholm
looked at Wickram. "Do you think it could be
deactivated, sir?"

"I honestly don't know, Lieutenant. I have powerful suspicions, but I just don't know. I would
imagine that this lies more in your field than
mine. Electronics, I mean. I know how to build

those damned weapons but I know nothing about those fancy triggering devices."

"Neither do I. Not without knowing how they work. For that I'd have to see the blueprint, a diagrammatic layout. You said you had powerful suspicions. What suspicions, sir?"

"I suspect that it can't be deactivated. In fact, I'm certain the process is irreversible. The second suspicion is also a certainty. I'm damn sure that I'm not going to be the one to try."

"That makes two of us. So what other options are open to us?"

Benson said, "May a total ignoramus venture an opinion? Why don't we take it to some safe place a hundred miles away and dump it at the bottom of the deep blue sea?"

"A tempting thought, Professor," Denholm said, "but not a very practicable one. It is, of course, a hundred percent certain that this triggering device is battery powered. The latest generation of Nife cells can lie dormant for months, even years, and still spring smartly to attention when called on to do their duty. You can't declare a whole area of the Mediterranean off-limits to all shipping for years to come."

"I prefaced my suggestion by saying that I was an ignoramus. Well, another doubtlessly ludicrous suggestion: we take it to the selfsame spot and detonate it."

Denholm shook his head. "I'm afraid that still leaves us with a couple of problems. The first is, how are we going to get it there?"

"We take it there."

"Yes. We take it there. Or we set out to take it there. Then somewhere en route the ticking stops. Then the triggering device cocks its ear and says, 'Aha! What's this I hear? Ship's engines,' and detonates. There wouldn't be even a second's warning."

"Hadn't thought of that. We could—I say this hopefully—tow it there."

"Our little friend is still listening and we don't know and have no means of knowing how sensitive its hearing is. Engines, of course, would set it off. So would a generator. A derrick winch, even a coffee grinder in the galley, might provide all the impulse it requires."

Talbot said, "You came all the way up to the bridge, Jimmy, just to spread sweetness and light, your own special brand of Job's comfort?"

"Not quite, sir. It's just that a couple of ideas occurred to me, one of which will have occurred to you and one you probably don't know about. Getting the bomb to its destination would be easy enough. We use a sailing craft. Lots of them hereabouts. Aegean luggers."

Talbot looked at Hawkins. "One can't think of everything. I forgot to mention, sir, that in addition to being a student of ancient Greek language and literature, Lieutenant Denholm is also a connoisseur of the small craft of the Aegean. Used to spend all his summers here—well, until we nabbed him, that is."

"I wouldn't begin to know how to sail those

luggers or caïques, in fact I couldn't even sail a dinghy if you paid me. But I've studied them, yes. Most of them come from the island of Samos and the Turkish port of Bodrum. Before the war—the First World War, that is—they were all sailing craft. Nowadays, they're nearly all engined, most of them with steadying sails. But there are quite a few with both engines and a full set of sails. Those are the *Trehandiri* and *Perama* types and I know there are some in the Cyclades. One of those would be ideal for our purposes. Because they have shallow keels, a minimum draft and no ballast they are almost useless performers to windward, but that wouldn't matter in this case. The prevailing wind here is northwest and the open sea lies to the southeast."

"Useful information to have," Talbot said. "Very useful indeed. You wouldn't happen to know anyone with such a craft?"

"As a matter of fact I do."

"Good God! You're as useful as your information." Talbot broke off as Van Gelder entered the bridge. "Duty done, Number One?"

"Yes, sir. Andropulous was a bit reluctant to go. So were Alexander and Aristotle. In fact, they point-blank refused to go. Infringement of their liberties as Greek civilians or some tosh to that effect. Demanded to know on whose orders. I said yours. Demanded to see you. I said in the morning. More outrage. I didn't argue with them, just called up McKenzie and some of his merry men, who removed them forcibly. I told McKenzie not to post any guards, just lock the doors and pocket the keys. You're going to hear from the Greek government about this, sir."

"Excellent. Wish I'd been there. And the girls?"

"Sweet reason. No problem."

"Fine. Now, Jimmy, you said a couple of ideas had occurred to you. What was the second one?"

"It's about the second problem that the professor raised. The detonation. We could, of course, try sympathetic detonation by dropping a depth charge on it but as we would be in the immediate vicinity at the time I don't think that would be a very good idea."

"Neither do I. So?"

"The Pentagon could have the answer. Despite feeble denials to the contrary, everyone knows that the Pentagon controls NASA—the National Aeronautics and Space Administration. NASA, in turn, is supposed to administer the Kennedy Space Center. 'Supposed' is the operative word. They don't. The center is operated by EG&G, a major defense contractor. EG&G—Dr. Wickram will know much more about this than I do—oversees such things as nuclear-weapons tests and the so-called Star Wars. More importantly, they are developing, or have developed, what they call the krytron, a remote-controlled electronic-impulse trigger that can detonate nuclear weapons. A word from the admiral in the ear of the Pentagon might work wonders."

Hawkins cleared his throat. "This little tidbit of

information, Lieutenant. It will, of course, like your other tidbits, be in the public domain?"

"It is, sir."

"You astonish me. Most interesting, most. Could be a big part of the answer to our problem, don't you agree, Commander?" Talbot nodded. "I think we should act immediately on this one. Ah! The very man himself."

Myers had just entered, carrying a piece of paper, which he handed to Talbot. "Reply to your latest query to the Pentagon, sir."

"Thank you. No, don't go. We'll have another message to send them in a minute." Talbot handed the paper to Hawkins.

"'Security at bomber base,'" Hawkins read, "'believed to be 99.99 percent effective. But cards on the table. However unlikely, there may be one chance in ten thousand that security has been penetrated. This could have been that one chance.' Well, isn't that nice. Absolutely useless piece of information of course.

"'Plane carried fifteen H-bombs of fifteen megatons each and three atom bombs, all three equipped with timing devices.' Well, that's just fine. So now we have three of those ticking monsters to contend with."

"With any luck, just one," Talbot said. "Sonar picks up only one. Extremely unlikely that all three would be ticking in perfect unison. Point's academic, anyway. One or a hundred, the big boys would still go up."

"Identified by size, they say," Hawkins went on

99

"'Sixty inches by six.' Pretty small for an atom bomb, I would have thought. Four thousand kilotons. That's a lot. Dr. Wickram?"

"By today's standards, peanuts. Less than half the size of the Hiroshima bomb. If the bomb has the dimensions they say, then it's very large for such a small explosive value."

"It goes on to say that they're designated for marine use. I suppose that's a fancy way of saying that they are mines. So your guess was right, Dr. Wickram."

"Also explains the size of the bomb. Quite a bit of space will be taken up by the timing mechanism and it will have to be weighted to give it negative buoyancy."

"The real sting comes in the tail," Hawkins said. "'When the ticking stops, the timing clock has run out and the firing mechanism is activated and ready to be triggered by mechanical stimulation,' by which I take it they mean ship's engines. So it looks as if you were right about that one, Van Gelder. Then, by way of cheerful farewell, they say that inquiries so far confirm that the timing mechanism, once in operation, cannot be neutralized and appears to be irreversible."

The last words were met with silence. No one had any comment to make, for the excellent reason that everyone had already been convinced of the fact.

"A message to the Pentagon, Myers. 'Urgently require to know state of development of the EG&G krytron'—that's k-r-y-t-r-o-n, isn't it, Lieutenant?—'nuclear detonation device.'" Talbot paused. "Add: 'If operating model exists essential dispatch immediately with instructions.' That do, Admiral?" Hawkins nodded. "Sign it Admiral Hawkins."

"We must be giving them quite some headaches in the Pentagon," Hawkins said in some satisfaction. "This should call for still more aspirin."

"Aspirins are not enough," Van Gelder said. "Sleepless nights are what are called for."

"You have something in mind, Van Gelder?"

"Yes, sir. They can have no idea of the really horrendous potential of the situation here at Santorini—the combination of all those megatons of hydrogen bombs, thermal plumes and volcanoes and earthquakes along the tectonic-plate boundaries and the possibly cataclysmic results. If Professor Benson here were to make a very brief précis of the lecture he gave us in the wardroom this evening it might give them something more to think about."

"You have an evil mind, Van Gelder. What a perfectly splendid suggestion. Uneasy will lie the heads along the Potomac this night. What do you think, Professor?"

"It will be a pleasure."

When Sublieutenant Cousteau, together with the two divers and their equipment, returned from Santorini, they found the *Ariadne* in virtual darkness. With the thought of the malevolent listening bug on the sea floor dominating every other in his mind, Talbot had sought Lieutenant Denholm's advice on the question of noise suppression. Denholm had not been half-heartened in his recommendations, with the result that the use of all mechanical devices on the ship, from generators to electric shavers, had been banned. Only essential lighting, radar, sonar and radio were functioning normally; all these could function equally well, as they had been designed to do, on battery power. The sonar watch on the ticking device in the crashed bomber was now continuous.

The two divers, Chief Petty Officer Carrington and Petty Officer Grant, were curiously alike, both about thirty, of medium height and compact build. Both were given to smiling often, a cheerfulness that in no way detracted from their almost daunting aura of competence. They immediately joined Talbot and Van Gelder in the wardroom.

"That's all I know about the situation down there," Talbot said, "and heaven knows it's little enough. I just want to know these three things— the extent of the damage, the location of this ticking noise and whether it's possible to remove this atom bomb or whatever, which I'm convinced in advance is impossible. You are aware of the dangers and you are aware that I cannot order you to do this. How does the prospect appeal, Chief?"

"It doesn't appeal at all, sir." Carrington was imperturbable. "Neither Bill Grant nor I am cast in the heroic mold. We'll walk very softly down there. You shouldn't be worrying about us, you should be worrying about what your crew are thinking. If we slip up they'll all join us in the wild blue yonder or whatever. I know you want to come down, sir, but is it really necessary? We're pretty experienced in moving around inside wrecks without banging into things, and explosives, you might say, are our business. Not, I admit, the kind of explosives you have down there but we know enough not to trigger a bomb by accident."

"And we might?" Talbot smiled. "You're very tactful, Chief. What you mean is that we might bang into things or kick a detonator on the nose or something of the kind. When you say 'necessary,' do you mean 'wise'? I refer to our diving experience or lack of it."

"We know about your diving experience, sir. You will understand that when we knew what we were coming into we made some discreet inquiries. We know that you have commanded a submarine and the lieutenant commander was your first lieutenant. We know you've both been through the HMS *Dolphin* submarine escape tower and that you've done more than a fair bit of free diving. No, we don't think you'll be getting in our way or banging things around." Carrington turned up his palms in acceptance. "What's your battery capacity, sir?"

"For essential and nonmechanical purposes, ample. Several days."

"We'll put down three weighted floodlights and suspend them about twenty feet above the bottom. That should illuminate the plane nicely. We'll have a powerful hand flash each. We have a small bag of tools for cutting, sawing and snipping. We also have an oxyacetylene torch, which is rather more difficult to use underwater than most people imagine, but as this is just a reconnaissance trip we won't be taking it along. The closed-circuit breathing is of the type we prefer, fifty-fifty oxygen and nitrogen with a carbon dioxide scrubber. At the depth of a hundred feet, which is what we will be at, we could easily remain underwater for an hour without any risk of either oxygen poisoning or decompression illness. That's academic. Provided there's access to the plane and the fuselage is not crushed, a few minutes should tell us all we want to know.

"Two points about the helmet. There's a rotary chin switch which you depress to activate an amplifier that lets us talk, visor to visor. A second press cuts it off. It also has a couple of sockets over the ears where you can plug in what is to all effects a stethoscope."

"That's all?"

"All."

"We can go now?"

"A last check, sir?" Carrington didn't have to specify what check.

Talbot lifted a phone, spoke briefly and replaced it.

"Our friend is still at work."

* * *

The water was warm and still and so very clear that they could see the lights of the suspended arc lamps even before they dipped below the surface of the darkened Aegean. With Carrington in the lead and using the marker-buoy anchor rope as a guide, they slid down fifty feet and stopped.

The three arc lamps had come to rest athwart the sunken bomber, sharply illuminating the fuselage and the two wings. The left wing, though still attached to the fuselage, had been almost completely sheared off between the inner engine and the fuselage and was angled back about thirty degrees from normal. The tail unit had been almost completely destroyed. The fuselage, or that part of it that could be seen from above, appeared to be relatively intact. The nose cone of the plane was shrouded in shadow.

They continued their descent until their feet touched the top of the fuselage, half walked, half swam until they reached the front of the plane, switched on their flashlights and looked through the completely shattered windows of the cockpit. The pilot and the copilot were still trapped in their seats. They were no longer men, just the vestigial remains of what had once been human beings. Death must have been instantaneous. Carrington looked at Talbot and shook his head, then dropped down to the seabed in front of the nose cone.

The hole that had been blasted there was roughly circular with buckled and jagged edges projecting outward, conclusive proof that the blast had been internal; the diameter of the hole was approximately five feet. Moving slowly and cautiously so as not to rip any of the rubber components of their diving suits, they passed in file into a compartment not more than four feet in height but almost twenty feet in length, extending from the nose cone to under the flight deck and then several feet beyond. Both sides of the compartment were lined with machinery and metal boxes so crushed and mangled that their original function was incomprehensible.

Two-thirds of the way along the compartment a hatch had been blasted upward. The opening led to a space directly behind the seats of the two pilots. Aft of this was what was left of a small radio room with a man who appeared to be peacefully sleeping leaning forward on folded arms, the fingers of one hand still on a transmitting key. Beyond this, four short steps led down to an oval door let into a solid-steel bulkhead. The door was secured by eight clamps, some of which had been jammed into position by the impact of the blast. A hammer carried by Carrington in his canvas bag of tools soon tapped them into a loosened position.

Beyond the door lay the cargo compartment, bare, bleak, functional and obviously designed for one purpose only, the transport of missiles. These were secured by heavy steel clamps which were in turn bolted to longitudinal reinforced steel beams let into the floor and sides of the fuselage.

There was oil mixed with the water in the compartment but even in the weird, swirling yellowish light they looked neither particularly menacing nor sinister. Slender, graceful, with either end encased in a rectangular metal box, they looked perfectly innocuous. Each contained fifteen megatons of high explosive.

There were six of those in the first section of the compartment. As a formality, and not because of any expectations, Talbot and Carrington applied their stethoscopes to each cylinder in turn. The results were negative, as they had known they would be; Dr. Wickram had been positive that they contained no timing devices.

There were also six missiles in the central compartment. Three of these were of the same size as those in the front compartment; the other three were no more than five feet in length. Those had to be the atom bombs. It was when he was testing the third of those with his stethoscope that Carrington beckoned to Talbot, who came and listened in turn. He didn't have to listen long. The two-and-a-half-second ticking sequence sounded exactly as it had in the sonar room.

In the aft compartment they went through the routine exercise of listening to the remaining six missiles and found what they had expected, nothing. Carrington put his visor close to Talbot's.

"Enough?"

"Enough."

* * *

"That didn't take you long," Hawkins said.

"Long enough to find out what we needed. Missiles are there, all present and correct as listed by the Pentagon. Only one bomb has been activated. Three dead men. That's all, except for the most important fact of all. The bomber crashed because of an internal explosion. Some kindly soul had concealed a bomb under the flight deck. The Pentagon must be glad that they added the faint possibility that there was one chance in ten thousand that security might be breached. The faint possibility came true. Raises some fascinating questions, doesn't it, sir? Who? What? Why? When? We don't have to ask where, because we already know that."

"I don't want to sound grim or vindictive," Hawkins said, "because I'm not. Well, maybe a little. This should cut the gentlemen in Foggy Bottom, or wherever, down to size and make them a mite more civil and cooperative in future. Not only is it an American plane that is responsible for the dreadful situation in which we find ourselves, but it was someone in America who was ultimately responsible. If they ever do discover who was responsible, and it's not outside the realm of possibility, it's going to cause an awful lot of red faces. I'd lay odds that the person responsible is an insider, a pretty high-up insider with free access to classified information, such as closely guarded secrets as to the composition of the cargo, the destination and the time of takeoff and arrival. Wouldn't you agree, Commander?"

"I don't see how it can be otherwise. Not a problem I'd care to have on my hands. However, that's *their* problem. We have an even bigger problem on our hands."

"True, true." Hawkins sighed. "What's the next step, then? In recovering this damn bomb, I mean."

"I think you should ask Chief Petty Officer Carrington, sir, not me. He and Petty Officer Grant are the experts."

"It's a tricky one, sir," Carrington said. "Cutting away a fuselage section large enough to lift the bomb through is straightforward enough. But before we could lift the bomb out we would have to free it from its clamps and this is where the great difficulty lies. Those clamps are made of high-tensile steel fitted with a locking device. For that we need a key and we don't know where the key is."

"It could be," Hawkins said, "that the key is held at the missile base where the bombs were due to be delivered."

"With respect, sir, I think that unlikely. Those clamps had to be locked at the Air Force base where they were loaded. So they would have to have a key there. I think it would be much easier and more logical if they just took the key with them. Trouble is, a key is a very small thing and that's a very big bomber indeed.

"If there's no key, there are two ways we can

remove that clamp. One is chemical, using either a metal softener or a corrosive. The metal softener is used by stage magicians who go in for spoon bending and suchlike."

"Magicians?" Hawkins said. "Charlatans, you mean."

"Whatever. The principle is the same. They use a colorless paste which has no effect on the skin but has the peculiar property of altering the molecular structure of a metal and making it malleable. A corrosive is simply a powerful acid that eats through steel. Lots of them on the market. But, in this case, both softeners and corrosives have one impossible drawback: you can't use them underwater."

Hawkins said, "You mentioned two ways of removing the clamp. What's the other?"

"Oxyacetylene torch, sir. Make short work of any clamp. It would also, I imagine, make even shorter work of the operator. Those torches generate tremendous heat and I should also imagine that anyone who even contemplates using an oxyacetylene torch on an atom bomb is an obvious candidate for the loony bin."

Hawkins looked at Wickram. "Comment?"

"No comment. Not on the unthinkable."

"I speak in no spirit of complaint, Carrington," Hawkins said, "but you're not very encouraging. What you are about to suggest, of course, is that we wait for the *Kilcharran* to come along and hoist the damn thing to the surface."

"Yes, sir." Carrington hesitated. "But there's a snag even to that."

"A snag?" Talbot said. "You are referring, of course, to the distinct and unpleasant possibility that the ticking might stop while the *Kilcharran's* winch engine is working overtime at hauling the bomber to the surface?"

"I mean just that, sir."

"A trifle. There are no trifles that the combined brainpower aboard the *Ariadne* can't solve." He turned to Denholm. "You can fix that, Lieutenant?"

"Yes, sir."

"How, sir?" There was a pardonable note of doubt if not outright disbelief in Carrington's voice. Lieutenant Denholm didn't look like the type of person who could fix anything.

Talbot smiled. "If I may say this gently, Chief, one does not question Lieutenant Denholm on those matters. He knows more about electronics than any man in the Mediterranean."

"It's quite simple, Chief," Denholm said. "We just couple up the combined battery power of the *Ariadne* and the *Kilcharran*. "The *Kilcharran's* winches are probably diesel-powered. We may or may not be able to convert it to electrical use. If we can't, it doesn't matter. We have excellent electrical anchor windlasses on the *Adriadne*."

"Yes, but—well, with one of your two anchors out of commission you'd start drifting, wouldn't you?"

"We wouldn't drift. A diving ship normally carries four splayed anchors to moor it precisely over any given spot on the ocean floor. We just tie up to the *Kilcharran*, that's all."

"I'm not doing too well, am I? One last objection, sir. Probably a feeble one. An anchor is only an anchor. This bomber and its cargo probably weigh over a hundred tons. I mean, it's quite a lift."

"Diving ships also carry flotation bags. We strap them to the plane's fuselage and pump them full of compressed air until we achieve neutral buoyancy."

"I give up," Carrington said. "From now on, I stick to diving."

"So we twiddle our thumbs until the *Kilcharran* arrives," Hawkins said. "But not you, I take it, Commander?"

"I think we'll have a look at the *Delos*, sir."

5

They had rowed about a mile when Talbot called up the *Ariadne*. He spoke briefly, listened briefly, then turned to McKenzie, who was at the tiller.

"Ship oars. The timing device is still at it, so I think we'll start the engine. Gently at first. At this distance I hardly think we'd trigger anything even if the bomb were activitated, but no chances. Course oh-nine-five."

There were nine of them in the whaler—Talbot, Van Gelder, the two divers, McKenzie and the four seamen who had rowed them so far.

After about forty minutes Van Gelder moved up into the bows with a portable six-inch searchlight, which, on such a clear night, had an effective range of over a mile. The searchlight was probably superfluous, for there was a three-quarter moon and Talbot, with his night glasses, had a clear bearing on the monastery and the radar station on Mount Elias. Van Gelder returned within minutes and handed the searchlight to McKenzie.

"Fine off the port bow, Chief."

"I have it," McKenzie said. The yellow buoy, in the light of both the moon and the searchlight, was clearly visible. "Do I anchor?"

"Not necessary," Talbot said. "No current that's worth speaking of, no wind. Just make fast to the buoy."

McKenzie did just that and the four divers slipped over the side, touching down on the deck of the *Delos* just over an hour after leaving the *Ariadne*. Carrington and Grant disappeared down the for'ard companionway while Talbot and Van Gelder took the after one.

Talbot didn't bother entering the after stateroom. The two girls had stayed there and he knew it would hold nothing of interest for him. He looked at the dead engineer, or the man whom Van Gelder had taken to be the engineer because of his blue overalls, and examined the back of his head carefully. The occiput had not been crushed and there were no signs of either bruising or blood in the vicinity of the deep gash in the skin of the skull. He rejoined Van Gelder, who had already moved into the engine room.

There was, of course, no smoke there now and very few traces of oil. In the light of their two powerful flashlights visibility was all that could be wished for and it took them only two minutes to carry out their examination; unless one is looking for some obscure mechanical fault there is very little to look for in an engine room. On their way out they opened up a toolbox and took out a long, slender chisel apiece.

They found the bridge to be all that they would have expected a bridge on such a yacht to be, with a plethora of expensive and largely unnecessary navigational aids, but in all respects perfectly innocuous. Only one thing took Talbot's attention, a wooden cupboard on the after bulkhead. It was locked, but on the understandable assumption that Andropulous wouldn't be having any further use for it Talbot wrenched it open with his chisel. It contained the ship's papers and ship's log, nothing more.

A door on the port side of the same bulkhead led to a combined radio room and chart room. The chart-room section held nothing that a chart room should not have had, including a locked cupboard, which Talbot opened in the same cavalier fashion he had used on the bridge; it held only pilot books and sailing directions. Andropulous, it seemed, just liked locking cupboards. The radio was a standard RCA. They left.

They found Carrington and Grant waiting for them in the saloon. Carrington was carrying what appeared to be a portable radio; Grant had a black metallic box about thirteen inches by sixteen inches and less than three inches thick. Carrington put his visor close to Talbot's.

"All we could find. Of interest, I mean."

"We have enough."

"Dispatch would appear to be the keynote of your investigations, Commander," Hawkins said. Glass in hand, he was seated across the wardroom table from Talbot. "I mean, you seem to have spent singularly little time on your, um, aquatic investigation."

"You can find out interesting things in a very short space of time, sir. Too much, for some people."

"You refer to our shipwrecked friends?"

"Who else? Five things, sir. Van Gelder was right; there were no signs of bruising or blood where the engineer had been gashed on the head. An examination of the engine room turned up no signs of protrusions, angle beams or sharp metallic corners that could have caused the injury. Circumstantial evidence, I know, but evidence that strongly suggest that the engineer was clobbered by a heavy metallic instrument. No shortage of those in an engine room. We have, of course, no clue as to the identity of the assailant.

"Secondly, I'm afraid the owner of the *Delos* has been guilty of telling you fibs, Admiral. He said he left the *Delos* because he was afraid that the reserve fuel tank might blow up. There is no such tank."

"Isn't that interesting. Does make things look a little black for Andropulous."

"It does a bit. He could always claim, of course,

that he knew nothing of the layout of the engine room and had always assumed that there had to be a reserve tank or that in a panic-stricken concern for the welfare of his beloved niece he had quite forgotten that there was no such tank. He's undoubtedly intelligent; we know he's a thespian of some note and could put up a spirited and convincing defense in court. But he'd have no defense against a further charge that the explosion was not due to natural causes, unless you regard the detonation of a bomb, almost certainly a plastic explosive, under the main fuel tank as being a natural cause."

"Well, well, well. One wonders how he'll talk his way out of this one. You're quite certain, of course?"

Van Gelder said, "The captain and I are developing quite some expertise on the effects of explosives on metal. In the bomber, the metal of the fuselage was blown outward: in this case, the metal of the fuel tank was blown inward."

"We are not explosives experts, sir," Talbot said. "But it would seem that Andropulous wasn't either." He nodded toward Carrington and Grant. "But those two gentlemen *are* experts. We were talking about it on the way back. They reckon that Andropulous—if it was Andropulous; it could have been Alexander or Aristotle—made an amateurish blunder. Whoever it was should have used what they call an inverted-beehive plastic explosive attached to the underside of the tank by a magnetic clamp, in which case more than ninety percent of the explosive charge would have been directed upward. It would seem that they didn't use such a device."

Hawkins looked at Carrington. "You can be sure of this, Chief?"

"As sure as can be, sir. We do know that he couldn't have used a beehive. The explosive charge would have been either flat, circular or cylindrical and in any of those cases the disruptive explosive power would have been uniformly distributed in all directions. Grant and I think he didn't deliberately sink the yacht but that he just, through ignorance, kind of accidentally blew a hole through the bottom."

"If it weren't for the three dead men, this could be almost amusing. As it is, one has to admit that life is full of its little ironies. What's that you've got in front of you there, Carrington?"

"Some sort of radio, sir. Took it from Alexander's cabin."

"Why did you take it?"

"Struck me as odd, sir, unusual, out of place, you might say. Every cabin is fitted with its own bulkhead radio—all probably fed from the central radio in the saloon. So why should he require this additional radio, especially when he had access to—and was probably the only user of—the much superior radio in his radio room?"

Talbot looked at Denholm. "Just a standard radio, is it?"

"Not quite." Denholm took the radio and examined it briefly. "A transceiver, which means it can transmit as well as receive. Hundreds of them around, thousands, most commonly as ship-to-shore radios in private yachts. Also used in geological and seismological work and construction building. Remote-control detonation." He paused and look around myopically. "I don't want to sound sinister but it could equally well be used to trigger off the detonator in an explosive device being carried by an American Air Force bomber."

There was a brief silence, then Hawkins said, "I don't want to complain, Denholm, but you do rather tend to complicate matters."

"I used the word 'could,' sir, not 'did.' On the whole, given the mysterious and inexplicable circumstances, I rather think I prefer the word 'did.' If that is the case it leads, of course, to even more mysteries. How did Andropulous or whoever know when, and from where, that bomber was leaving? How did he know its cargo? How did he know an explosive device was being smuggled aboard? How did he know the radio wavelength to set it off? And, of course, there's the why, why, why."

The silence was considerably longer this time. Finally, Hawkins said, "Maybe we're doing Andropulous an injustice. Maybe Alexander is the mastermind."

"Not a chance, sir." Van Gelder was definite. "Andropulous lied about the spare tank. He had connections with main centers of known gunrunning activities. The fact that Alexander, who unquestionably plays the role of sidekick, had the radio in his cabin is of no significance. I should imagine that Irene Charial might be in the habit of dropping in on her uncle occasionally and he wouldn't want her saying, 'Whatever are you doing with a spare radio in your cabin, Uncle?' I can hardly imagine her dropping in on Alexander at any time. So Alexander kept the radio."

"You mentioned the possibility of an insider at this Air Force base in America, sir," Talbot said. "I think we should be thinking in terms of a whole platoon of insiders. You will be composing messages for the Pentagon, Air Force Intelligence and the CIA? Suitably etched in acid. I think by this time they must be dreading the thought of another signal from the *Ariadne*. I don't see much point in your going to Washington and entering a popularity contest."

"The slings and arrows—well, we're accustomed to injustices. What do you have in that box?"

"Petty Officer Grant picked this up in Andropulous's cabin. Haven't opened it yet." Not without difficulty he undid two spring clips and lifted the lid. "Waterproof." He looked at the contents. "Means nothing to me."

Hawkins took the box from him, lifted out some sheets of paper and a paperback book, examined them briefly and shook his head. "Means nothing to me either. Denholm?"

Denholm shuffled through the papers. "In Greek, naturally. Looks like a list of names, addresses and telephone numbers to me. But I can't make sense of it."

"I thought you understood Greek?"

"I do. But I don't understand Grecian code. And this is what it's written in—a code."

"Code! Damn it to hell." Hawkins spoke with considerable feeling. "This could be urgent. Vital."

"It's more than likely, sir." Denholm looked at the paperback. "Homer's *Odyssey*. I don't suppose it's here just by coincidence. If we knew the connection between the poem and what's written on those sheets, then cracking the code would be child's play. But we don't have the key. That's locked away inside Andropulous's mind. Anagrams and word puzzles are not in my line of country, sir. I'm no cryptologist."

Hawkins looked moodily at Talbot. "You don't have a code cracker among this motley crew you have aboard?"

"To the best of my knowledge, no. And certainly not a Greek code cracker. Shouldn't be too difficult to find one, I should imagine. The Greek Defense Ministry and their Secret Service are bound to have some cryptologists on their staffs. Just a radio call and half an hour's flight away, sir."

Hawkins glanced at his watch. "Two A.M. All Godfearing cryptologist are tucked up in their beds by this time."

"So are all God-fearing admirals," Denholm said. "Besides, my friend Wotherspoon didn't mind being rousted out of bed an hour ago. Positively cheerful about it, in fact."

Talbot said, "Who, may I ask warily, is Wotherspoon?"

"Professor Wotherspoon. My friend with the Aegean lugger. You asked me to contact him, remember? Lives in Naxos, seven or eight hours' sail from here. He's on his way with the *Angelina*."

"Very civil of him, I must say. *Angelina*? Odd name."

"Better not let him hear you say that, sir. Name of his lugger. Ancient and honored Grecian name, some sort of classical goddess, I believe. Also the name of his wife. Charming lady."

"Is he, what shall we say, slightly eccentric?"

"All depends upon what you mean by eccentric. He regards the rest of the world as being slightly eccentric."

"A professor? What does he profess?"

"Archaeology. Used to. He's retired now."

"Retired? Oh, dear. I mean, have we any right to bring an elderly archaeologist into this?"

"Don't let him hear you say that either, Sir. He's not elderly. Old man left him a fortune."

"You warned him of the danger of course?"

"As directly as I could. Seemed amused. Said his ancestors fought at Agincourt and Crécy. Something to that effect."

"What's good enough for a retired archaeologist should be good enough for a Greek cryptologist,"

Hawkins said. "Not that I follow the logic of that. If you would be so good, Commander."

"We'll radio Athens right away. Two things, sir. I suggest we release Andropulous and his friends for breakfast and leave them free. We've got plenty on them, but as yet no conclusive proof, and the three A's—Andropulous, Aristotle and Alexander—are a close-mouthed and secretive lot and we can be certain they won't talk to us or give anything away. But they might, just might, talk among themselves. Lieutenant Denholm will lurk unobtrusively. They don't and won't, know that he speaks Greek as well as they do. Number One, would you tell McKenzie to warn the four seamen who were with us tonight that they are on no account to mention the fact that we were on the *Delos*. One other thing. The presence of the cryptographer, when he arrives, will not go unnoticed."

"He's not a cryptographer," Van Gelder said. "He will be a civilian electronics specialist who's come out to fix some abstruse electronic fault that only he can fix. Also gives a splendid reason for him to use Denholm's cabin while he gets on with his decoding."

"Well, thank you very much." Denholm smiled and turned to Talbot. "With the captain's permission I'd like to retire there right now and get some sleep before this imposter arrives."

"An excellent idea. Vice Admiral Hawkins, Professor Benson, Dr. Wickram, I suggest you follow his example. I promise you we'll give you a shake if anything untoward occurs."

"Another excellent idea," Hawkins said. "After our nightcap. *And* after you've sent your signal to Athens and I've composed a suitably stirring message to the Chairman of the Joint Chiefs of Staff in Washington."

"Stirring?"

"Certainly. Why should I be the only one suffering from insomnia? I shall tell him that we have every reason to believe that the bomber was carrying a smuggled explosive device aboard, that its detonation was triggered by a radio wave and that we have the miscreant responsible in our hands. Reason to believe, not proof. I shall name Andropulous. I shall want to know how he knew when and from where that bomber was taking off. How did he know what it was carrying? How could this explosive device have possibly been smuggled aboard? How did he know the radio wavelength to set it off? I shall suggest that our concern should be made immediately known to the White House, Air Force Intelligence, the CIA and the FBI. I will suggest that Andropulous has been provided with top-level, ultrasecret information from a very senior official. This should considerably narrow their field of search. I will further suggest that it seems very likely that the traitor is in his own fiefdom, the Pentagon."

"Stirring indeed. Laying it on the line, as you might say." Talbot paused. "It has occurred to you, Admiral Hawkins, that you might also be laying your own career on the line."

"Only if I'm wrong."

"Only if we're wrong."

"In the circumstances, a bagatelle. You would do exactly the same thing."

"Five o'clock, sir." Talbot woke in his sea cabin abaft the bridge to find Van Gelder bending over him. "The *Kilcharran* is three miles out."

"What's the latest word from sonar?"

"Still ticking away, sir. Captain Montgomery says he's going to shut down his engines in another half mile. Sees us clearly and reckons he'll come to a stop more or less alongside. He says that if he's going to overshoot he'll use a sea anchor or drop a stern anchor and if he stops short of us he'll send a crew with a rope. From the way he talks he seems to regard either possibility as a remote contingency. Doesn't seem the shy or bashful type."

"I gathered as much from the admiral. Has our cryptologist arrived?"

"Yes. Calls himself Theodore. Speaks perfect English but I suppose he's Greek. Installed in Denholm's cabin. Denholm himself is up in the wardroom trying to resume his slumbers." Van Gelder broke off to accept a sheet of paper from a seaman who had appeared in the doorway, glanced briefly at the message and handed it without a word to Talbot, who read it in turn, muttered something inaudible and swung his legs to the deck.

"He'll have to try to resume his slumbers later on. Tell him to join us in the admiral's cabin at once."

A pajama-clad Vice Admiral Hawkins, propped up on the pillows of his bunk, glowered at the message in his hand and passed it across to Denholm. "Pentagon. Unsigned. This krytron device you suggested."

"If I were the spluttering type, which I'm not, this would be a sure fire starter." Denholm reread the message. "'Understand krytron experimental device in hand. Endeavor expedite soonest clearance.' Gobbledygook, sir. Writer is ignorant or stupid or thinks he's clever. Very likely all three at once. What does he mean 'endeavor'? He can either do it or not. What does he mean 'understand'? He either knows or not. 'Expedite'? Means to try to hurry things along. The Pentagon don't expedite—they demand immediate compliance. Same goes for that meaningless word 'soonest.' Again, should be 'immediate.' Clearance by whom? The Pentagon can clear anything they want. What do they mean 'experimental'? Either it works or it doesn't. And doesn't the phrase 'in hand' have a splendid meaningless vagueness about it? Gobbledygook, sir."

"Jimmy's right sir," Talbot said. "It's insulting. Stalling for time. What they're saying in effect is that they're not going to entrust their latest toy to their closest ally because we'd flog it to the first Russian we came across."

"It's rich," Denholm said. "It's really wonderful. The Americans positively force their Stinger surface-to-air missiles on the rebels who are fighting the Marxist regime in Angola and the contras in Nicaragua. It's no secret that those guerrilla bands contain a fair proportion of characters who are just as undesirable as the dictatorial governments they're supposed to be fighting and who would have no hesitation in disposing of those sixty-thousand-dollar missiles, at a fraction of their cost, to any passing terrorists, who, in turn, would have no hesitation in loosing off one of those missiles at a passing Boeing 747, preferably one packed with five hundred American citizens. But that's perfectly O.K. for the American administration's ad hoc knee-jerk set of reactions that passes for their foreign policy. But it's unthinkable that they should allow the krytron into the hands of their oldest ally. It makes me sick."

"It makes me mad," Hawkins said. "Give them a lesson on clear and unequivocal English. 'Unsigned message received. Meaningless mumbo jumbo designed to stall and delay. Demand immediate, repeat immediate, repeat immediate dispatch of krytron or immediate, repeat immediate, repeat immediate explanation of why not available. Sender of message and person responsible for delay in clearance will be held directly responsible for possible deaths of thousands. Can you not imagine the worldwide reaction when it is learned not only that America is responsible for this potential disaster but that it was almost certainly caused by treason in the highest American military echelons. A copy of this message is being sent directly to the President of the United States.' Will that do?"

"You could have pitched it a bit more strongly, sir," Talbot said, "but I'd have to spend the rest of the night thinking how. You spoke earlier of sleepless heads along the Potomac. I think we should now talk of heads rolling along the Potomac. If I were you, sir, I'd keep clear of Washington for some little time, by which I mean the rest of your life." He rose. "The *Kilcharran* will be alongside in a few minutes. I assume you are in no hurry to meet Captain Montgomery?"

"You assume right. There is no charity in me." He looked at his watch. "Five-thirteen. My respects to the captain and ask him to join me for breakfast at, say, eight-thirty. In my cabin here."

Captain Montgomery, whether by luck or design—design, Talbot was certain—brought the *Kilcharran* alongside the *Ariadne* with faultless precision. Talbot stepped across the two gunwales—they were almost exactly of a height—and made his way up to the bridge. Captain Montgomery was a tall, burly character with a jutting black beard, white teeth, a slightly hooked nose and humorous eyes and, in spite of the immaculately cut uniform and four golden rings on either cuff, could easily have passed for a well-to-do and genial eighteenth-century Caribbean pirate. He extended a hand.

"You'll be Commander Talbot, of course." The voice was deep, the Irish brogue unmistakable. "You are welcome aboard. Has there been any further deterioration in the situation?"

"No. The only deterioration possible, Captain, is one I don't care to imagine."

"Indeed. I shall be sadly missed in the Mountains of Mourne. We're great ones for the lamentations, the weepings and the wailings in the Mountains of Mourne. Is this atom bomb, or whatever, still ticking away?"

"It is. I suppose you might call it a deterioration when the ticking stops. You shouldn't have come here, Captain. You should have nipped into the Gulf of Corinth—you might have stood a chance there."

"Not to be thought of for a moment. Nothing to do with heroics—heroics are for those epics they make in Hollywood—or the fact that I couldn't live with myself. I just couldn't stand the thought of what that man would say."

"You'll be referring to Vice Admiral Hawkins?"

"The very same. Maligning and blackening my character as usual, I daresay?"

"Hardly." Talbot smiled. "He did, mind you, make some casual remark about you being allergic to certain naval regulations. He also said you're the best in the business."

"Aye. A fair man and a bloody good admiral— but don't tell him I said so. I suggest coffee in my cabin, Commander, and perhaps you'll be kind enough to tell me all you know."

"That shouldn't take long."

"Eleven P.M.," the President said. "What's the time over there?"

"Six A.M. There's a seven-hour time difference."

"A very forthright character, this Admiral Hawkins." The President gazed thoughtfully at the two dispatches lying on his desk. "You know him, of course?"

"Pretty well, sir."

"An able man, General?"

"Exceptionally so."

"He also appears to be an exceptionally tough s.o.b."

"That's undoubtedly true, sir. But then you have to be to command the NATO Mediterranean sea forces."

"Do you know him, John?" This was to John Heiman, the Defense Secretary, the only other person present.

"Yes. Not as well as the general, but well enough to agree with the general's assessment."

"Pity I never met him. Who selected him for the job, General?"

"The usual NATO committee."

"You were on it, of course?"

"Yes. I was the chairman."

"The man with the casting vote?"

"No casting vote. The decision was unanimous."

"I see. He—well, he seems to have rather a low opinion of the Pentagon."

"He doesn't exactly say that. But he does appear to have a low opinion, deep suspicions if you like, of a person or persons in the Pentagon."

"Puts you in a rather unhappy position. I mean, there must be some stirrings in the Pentagon."

"As you say, Mr. President, a few ruffled feathers. Some are hopping mad. Others are giving the matter serious consideration. Generally, you could call it an air of quiet consternation."

"Are you, personally, prepared to lend any credence to this outrageous suggestion? Or what appears to be outrageous?"

"Think the unthinkable? I don't have any option, do I? Every instinct says no, this cannot be, those are all my friends and colleagues of many years standing, all honorable men. But instinct is a fallible guide, Mr. President. Common sense and what little knowledge of history I have tells me that every man has his price. I have to investigate. The inquiry is already under way. I thought it prudent not to involve the intelligence arms of the four services. So, the FBI. The Pentagon does not care to be investigated by the FBI. It's an extremely difficult and delicate situation, sir."

"Yes. One can hardly go up to an admiral of the fleet and ask him what he was doing on the night of Friday the thirteenth. I wish you luck." The President looked at one of the papers before him.

"Your message re the krytron that provoked Hawkins's ire must have been badly handled."

"It was. Very badly. The matter has been attended to."

"This krytron device. Is it operational?"

"Yes."

"Been sent?" The general shook his head, the President pressed a button and a young man entered. "Take this message for the general here. 'Krytron device en route. Would greatly appreciate up-to-date assessment of existing problems and measures being taken. Fully appreciate extreme gravity, dangers and complexities of the situation. I personally guarantee total and immediate, repeat immediate, repeat immediate support and cooperation in all measures undertaken.' That should do it. Sign my name."

"I hope he appreciates the three 'immediates,'" the general said.

"Eight-forty, sir," McKenzie said. "Admiral's apologies, but he'd like to see you. He's in his cabin with Captain Montgomery."

Talbot thanked him, rose, washed the sleep from his face and eyes and made his way to the admiral's quarters. A shirt-sleeved Hawkins beckoned him to join him and Montgomery at the breakfast table.

"Coffee? Sorry to disturb you." Hawkins looked remarkably fresh, rested and relaxed and was attacking his breakfast with some gusto. "But Captain Montgomery has been reporting the state of progress and I thought you might like to hear it. Incidentally, our friend the timing device is still ticking merrily away."

"We are making progress," Montgomery said. "Slow but steady—slow, because the presence of what the admiral calls your friend the timing device does have a rather inhibitory effect and we're probably taking some quite needless precautions as far as acoustic levels are concerned. But we're dealing with a devil we don't know and we're paying the devil more than his due. Our own sonar is now locked on to this device and the sonar room has suddenly become the focal center of interest in the *Kilcharran.*

"We have achieved two things. First, by coupling up the battery resources of our two vessels we have ample electric power to lift this wreck. Your young Lieutenant Denholm looks and talks like a character out of P. G. Wodehouse, but he unquestionably knows his stuff. Your engineer officer, McCafferty, is no slouch either and neither is mine. Anyway, no problem. Secondly, we've cut away the port wing of the bomber."

"You've what?" Talbot said.

"Well." Montgomery sounded almost apologetic. "It was three parts torn away in any case and I figured that neither you nor the U.S. Air Force would have had any further use for it. So I had it burnt off." Despite his faint air of apology, it was quite clear that Montgomery had no regrets about what had been a wholly unilateral decision; as the only expert on the spot, he had no intention of consulting anybody. "A difficult decision and a tricky operation. No one, as far as I know, has ever before cut away the wing of a submerged big jet. That's where the fuel tanks are located, and though it seemed likely that the partial tearing away of the wing had also ruptured the fuel lines and spilled the fuel, there was no way of being sure and no one has ever come up against the problem of what happens when an oxyacetylene jet meets a fuel tank underwater. But my men were very careful. There was no fuel and so no trouble. And now, at the present moment, my men are securing flotation bags and lifting slings to the plane.

"Removing this wing gives us two advantages, one minor, one major. The minor one is that with the wing and two very heavy jet engines gone we have that much less to lift, although I'm certain we could have lifted the whole lot without trouble. The major one is that the wing, had it been left there, would have snagged on the underside of the *Kilcharran* as it surfaced and tilted the fuselage, maybe to so acute an angle as to make access to this damned bomb difficult or impossible."

"Very well done, Captain," Hawkins said. "But surely there's still one problem. When the bomber surfaces, isn't the weight of the remaining wing and its two engines going to tilt it just as far in the other direction?"

Montgomery smiled in a kindly and tolerant

fashion which any average person would have found more than mildly infuriating.

"No problem," Montgomery said. "We're also securing floation bags under that wing. When the fuselage surfaces, the wings will still be underwater—you know how low wings are set on a modern jet. In the first stage of surfacing, only the top of the fuselage will be above water level. When we cut away a rectangular section over where the bomb is located I want as much water as possible below that section to dissipate the heat of the oxyacetylene torches. After we've made that hole in the top we'll lift the fuselage high enough to drain most of the water from it."

"How long will it take to inflate the bags and haul the plane to the surface?"

"An hour or two. I don't know."

"An hour or two?" Hawkins made no attempt to conceal his surprise. "I should have thought a few minutes. You don't know, you say. I would have thought those things could have been pretty closely calculated."

"Normally, yes." Montgomery's air of massive restraint was on a par for provocation with his kindly tolerance. "But normally we'd use powerful diesel compressors. Out of deference to the little lady lying on the sea floor, no diesel. We will use electricity but only a fraction of the power. So, an indeterminate period. Do you think I could have some more coffee?" Montgomery, clearly, regarded the conversation as over.

Van Gelder knocked on the opened door and

entered, a message slip in his hand. He handed it to Hawkins.

"For you, Admiral. Came in a couple of hours ago. Not urgent, so I didn't think it worth waking you for it."

"A wise decision, my boy." Hawkins read it, smiled broadly and handed it to Talbot, who glanced at it, smiled in turn and read it out aloud.

"Well, well," Talbot said. "Hobnobbing with Presidents. Perhaps, after all, sir, you could walk down Pennsylvania Avenue without being clapped in irons or whatever they do to you over in those parts. More importantly, you have the krytron and this splendid pledge of cooperation. Your indignation—the less charitable would call it a calculated gamble—has paid off. I like the 'repeat immediate' bit. The President would appear to have a sense of humor."

"He would indeed. One has to be grateful to him for intervening personally. Very, very satisfactory. I note that he requires information. Would you, please?"

"Naturally. Emphasis, of course, on the gravity and the dangers?"

"Of course."

"Another item of news, sir," Van Gelder said to Talbot. "I've just had a rather intriguing chat with Irene Charial."

"I can well imagine that. Andropulous and company, of course, are now at liberty. How are they this fine morning?"

"Glowering a bit, sir. At least Andropulous and

Alexander were. But the cook was in fine form and they seemed to be thawing a bit when I left them chattering away in Greek with Denholm sitting among them and not understanding a word they were saying. Irene wasn't there."

"Oh? So, naturally, you hurried up to my cabin to inquire after her health."

"Naturally. I knew that was what you would want me to do, sir. She didn't look as if she had slept too well and admitted as much. Seemed worried, apprehensive even. At first she was rather reluctant to talk about what was bothering her. Misplaced loyalty, I should say."

"I would say so, too," Talbot said. "If, that is, I knew what you were talking about."

"Sorry. Turned out she wanted to know if Uncle Adam had been sending any radio messages. It seems—"

"Uncle Adam?"

"Adamantios Andropulous. Or, as we know him, Spyros. Seems that she and her pal Eugenia —both sets of parents live in Piraeus, the two girls are at the university in Athens—were in the habit of phoning home every night. She wanted their parents to know that they had had an accident, were safely aboard a Royal Navy ship and would be home soon."

"I hope she's right," Hawkins said.

"Me, too, sir. I told her no messages had been sent and suggested that if Uncle was a businessman—I thought it better not to mention that we already knew he was a multimillionaire businessman—he might naturally tend to be secretive and that he might also be reluctant to broadcast the fact that he had lost his yacht through what might have been his own fault. She said that was no excuse for not informing the next of kin of the three crew members of the *Delos* who had died. I asked her if she had raised the question with him and she said no. She was a bit evasive on this point. I gather she either doesn't know very much about Uncle Adam or doesn't care very much about what she does know." Van Gelder produced a paper from his pocket. "I told her to write a message and I would see it was sent."

Talbot looked at the paper. "It's in Greek. Perhaps this Uncle Adam—"

"We share the same nasty, suspicious mind, sir. I called Jimmy from the breakfast table. Quite innocent, he says."

"I have a better idea. Take the two young ladies to the radio room. It's a simple matter to lock into the telephone land lines through the Piraeus radio station. They can talk direct to their folks."

"With Jimmy just happening to be there?"

"We share, as you say, the same nasty, suspicious minds. Before you do that, however, I think we'll go and see how our latest recruit is getting on."

"Ah! Our resident cryptologist. Theodore."

Talbot nodded. "After we've seen him and the young ladies have finished their calls I want you to take Irene Charial aside. It would seem that she and her uncle are less than soul mates and, of course, she will be feeling suitably grateful to you for having permitted her to speak to her folks. Find out what you can about Andropulous. Find out what she thinks of him. See what you can discover about his business or businesses. And it would be very interesting to know where his travels take him—I'm not talking about his yacht cruises when she is with him—and why they take him there."

"A pleasure, sir."

Theodore was a cheerful, plump man in his late forties, with a pale face and thick horn-rimmed glasses, those last a very probable consequence of having spent a lifetime pouring over abstruse codes.

"You have come to check on my progress, gentlemen. I am making some, I'm happy to report. Took me quite some time to find the key, the connection between the code and the *Odyssey*. Since then, it's been straightforward. These sheets are in three sections and I'm now about two-thirds of the way through the first one."

"Found anything of interest?" Talbot said.

"Interesting? Fascinating, Captain, fascinating. Statements of his accounts, bank holdings, if you like. He has his money 'stashed' away— 'stashed' is the word?—all over the world, it seems. As a matter of interest, I'm totting up the sum of his holdings as I go along. He's made it very easy for me, everything is in the U.S. dollars. So far, let me see it, it's two-eighty. Yes, two-eighty. Dollars."

"A man could retire on that," Van Gelder said.

"Indeed. Two-eighty. Followed by six zeros."

Talbot and Van Gelder looked at each other in silence, then bent forward over Theodore's shoulders to look at the figures he had added up. After some seconds they straightened, looked at each other again, then bent forward once more.

"Two hundred and eighty million dollars," Talbot said. "On that you *could* retire, Vincent."

If I scraped and pinched a bit, I might manage. Do you know where those bank accounts are kept, Theodore? Cities, countries, I mean."

"Some I do, because he's given names and addresses, some I don't. For the second lot, he may have another code which I don't have or he just knows them by heart. By heart, I would guess. I have no means of knowing where at least half the accounts are. Just the amounts, that's all."

"Could you show us some of those?" Talbot said.

"Of course." Theodore pointed to some entries, flipped over several pages and indicated several more. "Just amounts, as I said. As you see, there's a different capital letter after each entry. They mean nothing to me. Maybe they do to Andropulous."

Talbot leafed through the pages again. "Five letters, just five, recur regularly—Z, W, V, B and G. Well, now. If you were a thrifty citizen and wanted a safe piggy bank secure from the prying eyes of nasty parties such as police and income-tax authorities, which country would you choose?"

"Switzerland."

"I think the same far from original thought had occurred to Andropulous—for at least half his assets. Z for Zurich. W? Winterthur, perhaps. V? Offhand, I don't know about that one."

"Vevey?" Van Gelder said. "On Lake Geneva?"

"I don't think so. Hardly what you might call an international banking center. Ah! I have it. Not in Switzerland, but it might as well be. Vaduz. Liechtenstein. I don't know much about those things but I understand that once cash disappears into the vaults of Vaduz it never surfaces again. B could be Berne or Basle—Andropulous would know, of course. G has to be Geneva. How am I doing, Number One?"

"Splendidly. I'm sure you're right. I hardly like to point out, sir, that we still don't have the names and addresses of those banks."

"True. We still have names and addresses of other banks. You have a list of those cities where those banks are located?"

"I don't have to," Theodore said. "I have it in my head. They're all over the place, west, east and in between. Places as different as Miami, Tijuana, Mexico City, Bogotá in Colombia, Bangkok, Islamabad in Pakistan, Kabul in Afghanistan. Why anyone should want to hide away money in Kabul is quite beyond me. Country is torn by war and the Russians occupy and control the capital."

"Andropulous would appear to have friends everywhere," Talbot said. "Why should the poor Russians be left out in the cold. Is that the lot?"

"Quite a few other places," Theodore said. "Mostly smaller accounts. One exception, though. The biggest deposit of the lot."

"Where?"

"Washington, D.C."

"Well, now." Talbot was silent for a few minutes. "What do you make of that, Number One?"

"I think I've just about stopped making anything out of anything. My mind has kind of taken a leave of absence. But my eyes are still working, in a fashion, you might say. I think I see a faint light at the end of the tunnel."

"I think if we think a bit more it might turn into a searchlight. How much money?"

"Eighteen million dollars."

"Eighteen million dollars," Van Gelder mused. "Even in Washington, D.C., a man could buy a lot with eighteen million dollars."

6

The *Angelina*, to put it kindly, was a rather striking-looking craft. An eighty-tonner built of pinewood from the forests of the island of Samos, it had a dazzling white hull which contrasted strongly—some would have said violently—with its vermilion gunwale. Wide of beam and low in the water amidships, it had a pronounced flare aft and fore, a curved stem that projected high above the gunwale. As a sailing boat, it was well equipped with a standing-lug main and balance-lug foresail, together with two jibs. Had it been left at that, as it had originally ben built, the *Angelina*, a typical example of the *Trehandiri* class, would have been not only striking but downright handsome. Unfortunately, it had not been left at that.

The owner, Professor Wotherspoon, although a self-avowed traditionalist, was also strongly attached to his creature comforts. Not content with converting the craft's very considerable hold—it was, after all, originally constructed as a cargo vessel—into cabins and bathrooms, he had constructed on the deck a bridge, saloon and gallery which, while admittedly functional, detracted notably from the overall aesthetic effect.

Shortly before ten 'clock in the morning, the *Angelina*, almost slack-sailed and ghosting along under a Meltemi that hardly rated as a zephyr, tied up along the starboard side of the *Ariadne*. Talbot, accompanied by Denholm, climbed down a rope ladder to greet the owner.

The first impression that Talbot had of Wotherspoon was that he didn't look a bit like a professor or an archaeologist, but then, he had to admit, he had no idea what a professor or archaeologist was supposed to look like. He was tall, lean, shock-haired and deeply tanned. With his humorous manner and colloquial speech, he was the last person one would expect to find wandering through the groves of academe. He was certainly not more than forty years old. His wife, with auburn hair and laughing hazel eyes, was at least ten years younger and was also, it seemed, an archaeologist.

Introductions effected by Denholm, Talbot said, "I appreciate this very much, Professor. Very kind of you to come. Not to say very gallant. You appreciate that there is a fair chance that you might find yourself prematurely in another world? Lieutenant Denholm did explain the dangers to you?"

"In a cautious and roundabout fashion. He's become very tight-lipped since he joined the Senior Service."

"I didn't join. I was dragooned."

"He did mention something about vaporization. Well, one gets a bit tired of studying ancient history. Much more interesting to be a part of the making of it."

"It might be a very short-lived interest indeed. Does Mrs. Wotherspoon share your short-lived interests?"

"Angelina, please. We had to entertain a very prim and proper Swiss lady the other day and she insisted on addressing me as Madam Professor Wotherspoon. Ghastly. No, I can't say I share all of my husband's more extravagant enthusiasms. But, alas, he does have one professorial failing. He's horribly absentminded. Someone has to look after him."

Talbot smiled. "A fearful thing for so young and attractive a lady to be trapped for life. Again, thank you both very, very much. I should like it if you would join us for lunch. Meantime, I'll leave Lieutenant Denholm to explain the full horrors of the situation to you—especially the ones you'll encounter across the lunch table."

"Gloom and despondency," Van Gelder said. "It ill becomes one so young and beautiful to be gloomy and despondent. What *is* the matter, Irene?"

Irene Charial gazed out morosely over the taffrail of the *Ariadne*. "I am not, Lieutenant Commander Van Gelder, in the mood for flattery."

"Vincent. Flattery is an insincere compliment. How can the truth be flattery? But you're right about the word 'mood.' You are in a mood. You're worried, upset. What's troubling you?"

"Nothing."

"Being beautiful doesn't mean you're above telling fibs. You could hardly call that flattery, could you?"

"No." A fleeting smile touched the green eyes. "Not really."

"I know this is a very unpleasant situation you find yourself in. But we're all trying to make the best of it. Or did something your parents say upset you?"

"You know perfectly well that that's not true." Van Gelder also knew it. Denholm had reassured him on that point.

"Yes, that's so. You were hardly in a cheerful frame of mind when I first met you this morning. Something worries you. Is it so dreadful a secret that you can't tell me?"

"You've come here to pry, haven't you?"

"Yes. To pry and probe. Crafty, cunning, devious questions to extract information from you that you don't know you're giving away." It was Van Gelder's turn to look morose. "I don't think I'm very good at it."

"I don't think you are either. That man sent you, didn't he?"

"What man?"

"Now you're being dishonest. Commander Talbot. Your captain. A cold man. Distant. Humorless."

"He's neither cold nor distant. And he's got a very considerable sense of humor."

"Humor. I don't see any signs of it."

"I'm beginning not to be surprised." Van Gelder had stopped smiling. "Maybe he thought it would be wasted on you."

"Maybe he's right." She appeared not to have taken offense. "Or maybe I just don't see too much to laugh about at the moment. But I'm right about the other thing. He's remote, distant. I've met people like him before."

"I doubt it very much. In the same way that I doubt your power of judgment. You don't seem to be very well equipped in that line."

"Oh." She grimaced. "Flattery and charm have flown out the window, is that it?"

"I don't flatter. I've never claimed to have charm."

"I meant no harm. Please. I see nothing wrong with being a career officer. But he lives for only two things—the Royal Navy and the *Ariadne*."

"You're absolutely wrong." Van Gelder spoke without heat. "But how were you to know? John Talbot lives for only two things—his daughter and his son. Fiona, aged six, and Jimmy, aged three. He dotes on them. So do I. I'm their Uncle Vincent."

"Oh." She was silent for some moments. "And his wife?"

"Dead."

"I am sorry." She caught his arm. "To say I didn't know is no excuse. Go ahead. Call me a clown."

"I don't flatter, I don't charm—and I don't tell lies."

"But you do turn a pretty compliment." She took her hand away, leaned on the rail and looked out over the sea. After some time, she said, without looking around, "It's my Uncle Adam, isn't it?"

"Yes. We don't know him, we don't trust him and we think he's highly suspicious. You will forgive me talking about him in this fashion."

She had turned to face him. There was neither vehemence in her voice nor marked expression on her face—at most, a slight degree of bewilderment in both. "*I* don't know him, *I* don't trust him, and *I* think he's highly suspicious."

"If you don't know him, what on earth were you doing aboard his yacht?"

"I suppose that, too, seems suspicious. Not really. Three reasons, I would think. He's a very persuasive man. He seems to be genuinely fond of our family—my younger brother and sister and myself—for he is forever giving us presents, very expensive presents, too, and it seemed churlish to refuse his invitation. Then there was the element of fascination. I know practically nothing about him, or what his business activities are, or why he spends so much time in foreign countries. And, of course, perhaps both Eugenia and I are snobs at heart and were flattered by the invitation to go cruising on a very expensive yacht."

"Well, good enough reasons. But still not good enough to explain why you went with him if you dislike him."

"I didn't say I disliked him. I said I distrusted him. Not the same thing. And I didn't begin distrusting him until this trip."

"Why start now?"

"Alexander is why." She gave a mock shudder. "Would you trust Alexander?"

"Candidly, no."

"And Aristotle is almost as bad. The three of them spent hours talking together, usually in the radio room. Whenever Eugenia or I went near them, they stopped talking. Why?"

"Obvious, isn't it? They didn't want you to hear what they were talking about. Ever been with him abroad on his business trips?"

"Good heavens, no." She was genuinely startled at the idea.

"Not even on the *Delos*?"

"I've only been on the *Delos* once before. With my brother and sister. A short trip to Istanbul."

He was going to have a less than sensational report to make to his captain, Van Gelder reflected. She didn't know her uncle. She didn't know what his businesses were. She never traveled with him. And her only reason for distrusting him was that she distrusted Alexander, a feeling almost certainly shared by the majority of people who had ever met him. Van Gelder made one last try.

"Your mother's brother, of course?" She nodded. "What does she think of him?"

"She never speaks ill of him. But she never speaks ill of anyone. She's a wonderful lady, a wonderful mother, not simple or anything like that, just a very trusting person who could never bring herself to speak ill of anyone."

"She's obviously never met Alexander. Your father?"

"He never speaks of Uncle Adam either, but his silence is for very different reasons, if you follow me. My father is a very straight, very honest man, very clever, head of a big construction company, highly respected by everyone. But he doesn't speak of my uncle. I believe my father strongly disapproves of Uncle Adam or whatever businesses he runs. Or both. I don't believe they've talked in years." She shrugged and gave a faint smile. "Sorry I can't be of more help. You haven't learned anything, have you?"

"Yes, I have. I've learned I can trust you."

This time the smile was warm and genuine and friendly. "You don't flatter, you don't charm and you don't tell lies. But you *are* gallant."

"Yes," Van Gelder said. "I believe I am."

* * *

"Sir John," the President said, "you have put me in a most damnably awkward position. I speak, you understand, more in sorrow than in anger."

"Yes, Mr. President. I am aware of that and I'm sorry for it. It is, of course, no consolation for you to know that I am in a equally awkward situation" If Sir John Travers, the British ambassador to the United States, did indeed find himself in such a situation, he showed no signs of it. But then, Sir John was renowned throughout the diplomatic world for his savoir faire, his monolithic calm and his ability to remain wholly unruffled in the most trying and difficult situations. "I'm only the messenger boy. Grade one, of course."

"Who the hell is this fellow Hawkins anyway?" Richard Hollison, deputy director of the FBI, couldn't quite match Sir John's tranquil serenity but he had his obvious anger under tight control. "I don't think I care very much for having a foreigner telling the White House, the Pentagon and the FBI how to run their business."

"Hawkins is a vice admiral in the British Navy." The general was the fourth and only other person in the office. "An exceptionally able man. I cannot think of any United States naval officer whom I would sooner have in his place in these near-impossible circumstances. And I don't think I need point out that I am in the most awkward situation of all. I don't want to sound overly possessive but, hell, the Pentagon is *my* concern."

"Richard Hollison," Sir John said. "I've known you for some years now. I know your reputation for toughness is matched only by your reputation for fairness. Be fair in this case. Admiral Hawkins, as the general has just said, is in a position of having to cope with almost untenable circumstances which, as you are in a position to know better than most, involves making almost impossible decisions. He's not telling anyone how to run their business. In order to get a message to the President, without anyone in the government or the Pentagon seeing the message before the President, he elected to bypass the Pentagon and all the standard avenues of communication. Certainly the Pentagon knows they're already under investigation, but Hawkins didn't want anyone to know that he was pointing fingers in certain directions. If it is your intention to set a cat among the pigeons or less loose an eagle in the dovecote, you don't send a postcard in advance announcing your intentions."

"Yes, I accept that," Hollison said. "With weary resignation I accept it. But don't ask me to like it."

"Like it or lump it," the President said, "I accept it, too." He looked unenthusiastically at the paper before him on his desk. "It would appear that this Adamantios Andropulous, who is Hawkins's temporary guest—I could well imagine that Admiral Hawkins would use the term "guest" even if this unfortunate were clapped in irons in some shipboard dungeon—has an account with a Washington bank, name and address supplied, of some eighteen million dollars, and would we kindly make inquiries to see if he has been disbursing any of this of late and, if so, in what direction. I know this lies well within your capabilities, Richard. Point is, how long will it take?"

"All depends upon how many false names, how many dud companies, how much of the usual laundering paraphernalia are involved. He might well have a numbered account in Outer Mongolia. Unlikely, I admit, but you take my point. One hour, maybe three. Excuse me, Mr. President. Excuse me, gentlemen." Hollison left.

"The Army and the Marines will be pleased to learn—when they do learn of it—that Admiral Hawkins does not consider them worthy of his attention," the President went on. "Only the Air Force and the Navy. The Air Force I can, in the circumstances, understand. But it would be interesting to know why he has deemed the Navy to be deserving of his interests. He gives no indications on that score." The President sighed. "Maybe he doesn't even trust me. Or maybe he knows something that we don't know."

Sir John said placidly, "If that is the case—that he knows something we don't—I have little doubt that he'll tell us in the fullness of time."

* * *

The man under discussion in the White House was, at that moment, dwelling on precisely the same subject.

"Time's winged chariots, John. I forget the rest of the quotation but it's definitely on the wing." Leaning back in a comfortable armchair, a glass of frosted lime juice in his hand, Hawkins succeeded only in giving the impression of a man with all the time in the world.

"I think you might say, sir, that the patient is coming along as well as could be expected. Our carpenter is aboard the *Angelina*, building a cradle for the bomb according to the specifications the Pentagon gave us. There will be two hinged clamps to secure it in even the worst weather, which, as you can see for yourself, is the last thing we expect today."

"Indeed." The admiral looked through the window of his cabin. "The weather is all wrong, John. Considering the possibly apocalyptic and doom-laden task we have on hand, the least we could reasonably expect is high winds, torrential rain, thunder, lightning, tempests, tornadoes and all those other adverse weather conditions. But what do we have? A blistering July sun, a cloudless blue sky and the wine-dark seas without even a ripple to show for themselves. Downright disappointing. Also disappointing, not to say extremely disturbing, is the likelihood that if those zero-wind conditions persist, it'll take the *Angelina* a week to get even halfway to the horizon."

"I don't think we have to worry about that, sir. Weather conditions in the Cyclades between early July and mid-September are remarkably predictable. It's already eleven forty-five. Any minute now the Meltemi, the Etesian wind, should start up from the northwest. During the afternoon it reaches Force 5 or 6, sometimes even 7. Usually dies away in the evening but it has been known to last all night. The Meltemi will be ideally suited for the *Angelina*. Those luggers, as Denholm said, are hopeless windward sailors but in this case the wind will be directly astern of them and carry them down toward the Kasos Strait to the east of the eastern-most tip of Crete."

"Sounds fine, but, well, even *if* Montgomery manages to raise this bomber, *if* he manages to cut a hole in the fuselage without blowing us all to kingdom come, *if* he manages to extract the atom bomb and *if* he manages to secure it to the *Angelina*'s cradle, what happens if the thing detonates before he reaches the Kasos Strait?"

"Then that's it for Wotherspoon and his crew. For us, the risk is low. I've been talking to Dr. Wickram about this. He seems convinced of the inherent stability of the hydrogen bombs—after all, he does build the damn things. While he says it would be a hundred percent certain to go up if an atom bomb exploded alongside it, we mustn't overestimate the effects of a more remote explosive shock, even at a distance of a few miles. After all, those bombs did survive the effect of the explosion in the nose of the bomber and the impact of the plane hitting the water at high speed. Besides, the intervening miles of water—we hope there will be those intervening miles—should have a powerfully dampening effect."

"There'll be no such effect for those aboard the *Angelina*. What motivates a man like that, John? Obviously, he's incredibly brave—but, well, is he all right?"

"If you mean is he off his rocker, then we're all off our rockers. He's as sane as you or I. He's a romantic at heart, a born adventurer, a couple of hundred years ago he'd have been somewhere on the other side of the world building up the odd empire."

"Perhaps, but it's still a terrible thought that a man like that should die for us."

"He won't be dying for all of us. I'm going on the *Angelina*. So is Vincent Van Gelder."

Hawkins put down his glass and stared at him. "Do you know what you're saying? *I* know what you're saying and I think you've taken leave of your senses. Are you mad? You and Van Gelder? Quite mad?"

"Van Gelder insists on coming along. I insist on going. That's all there is to it."

"I absolutely forbid it."

"With the deepest respects, Admiral, you'll forbid me nothing. Did you honestly expect me to let him go out there and die alone? I would remind you that I am the captain of this ship and that at sea not even an admiral can take over from me or give orders which I consider to be to the detriment of this vessel."

"Insubordination!" Hawkins waved a dismissive hand at his lime juice. "Have we nothing stronger than this?"

"Naturally." Talbot went to the admiral's wine cupboard and prepared a drink while Hawkins gazed at a spot on the deck which was about a thousand miles away. "A large scotch and water. No ice."

"Thank you." Hawkins drained almost half the contents, muttering to himself.

"Can't hang me from the yardarm, though. It's my yardarm. You haven't yet met Angelina—Professor Wotherspoon's wife, I mean, not the lugger. But you will. I've invited them aboard for lunch. Young, rather lovely, nice sense of humor and dotty about her husband. She has to be—dotty, I mean—to do something she clearly doesn't want to do—that is, to go along from here with her husband and the bomb on the lugger."

"I'm sure I shall be delighted to make her acquaintance." Hawkins took another sip of his drink. "What's she got to do with the matter in hand?"

"She's not going with the bomb and the lugger. Neither is Wotherspoon, for that matter, or his two crew members. They remain aboard the *Ariadne*. Wotherspoon, of course, will have to be forcibly restrained, but that's no problem at all. Van Gelder and I will take the *Angelina* down through the Kasos Strait. Two small medals will suffice."

Hawkins was silent for quite some time, then said, "How are you going to pin on a couple of posthumous VCs or whatever when you're circling the earth in a vaporized orbit?"

"One problem at a time. We can't let the girl go."

"Good God, no. I'd never forgive myself. I never even started to think. I wonder—"

"We don't have room for three heroes aboard the *Angelina*. Someone has to take the *Ariadne* home again, remember? Well, that's the *Angelina*. Now, the *Kilcharran*. I've just been talking to Captain Montgomery. He's just given a couple of experimental tugs on the lifting slings and he reckons the bomber, with the help of the flotation bags, of course, is nearing a state of neutral buoyancy. Twenty minutes, half an hour at the most, and he's going to start to haul away. You won't want to miss that, sir."

"No, indeed. What did Walter de la Mare say— look your last on all things lovely every hour? This may be the last thing I'll ever see."

"I rather hope it doesn't come to that, sir. Apart from the lugger and the recovery of the bomber, we have to wait for three other things. The reaction to the message we sent to the President via our embassy in Washington, which might take quite some time. Even the most cooperative of banks—and banks almost by definition are secretive and detest the very thought of cooperation—

are going to be very reluctant to disclose any information about their important clients, because important clients don't like that sort of thing. Admittedly, Air Force generals and admirals are unlikely to be very important financially, but they are from the point of view of prestige and power and would, I should think, carry a disproportionate amount of clout. I do hope we haven't upset too many people over there. Then, and this I should expect very soon, there should be a reply from Greek Intelligence to our query asking for the complete list of places where Andropulous has conducted business, any kind of business, over the past few years. Then, of course, we await the arrival of this krytron device from America."

"Which may arrive any old time. I mean, we have no idea, have we? The Americans do have supersonic planes, don't they?"

"They have, but fighters only. And their nearest refueling point would be the Azores and I'm quite certain no fighter could fly the close to two thousand miles they'd have to travel to get there. Question of fuel capacity. Besides, it's not absolutely essential that we get this device before leaving with the bomb—always assuming, of course, that we do leave. We could always dump the bomb, drop a marker, warn all shipping to keep clear, wait for the krytron to arrive, return there and detonate the bomb."

"Much more satisfactory if it could all be done in one fell swoop." He thought for a moment, then smiled. "What's the time in Washington?"

"Four A.M., I think."

"Excellent, excellent. A short message. Ask them how it's been transported and what's the expected time of arrival. Give 'em something to do." Talbot lifted a phone and dictated the message.

"Haven't seen your second-in-command lately," Hawkins said. "I understand he was prying secrets loose from Andropulous's niece?"

"Vincent normally carries out his duties with efficiency and dispatch. When the duties involve Irene Charial, it seems to take a little longer."

"Not so many years ago it would have taken me a little longer myself. Ah!" Van Gelder had appeared in the doorway. "Just discussing you, young man. A difficult and protracted interview, I take it?"

"One treads delicately, sir. But she told me everything she knows." He looked reproachfully at Talbot. "I detect a trace of skepticism in your expression, sir. Unwarranted, I assure you. I trust her. I told her that you had sent me to try to trap her into making unwary and unguarded statements and unwittingly to betray herself. After that, we got along famously."

Talbot smiled. "Just another way of being devious. What does she know?"

"Nothing. I guarantee you'd come to the same conclusion, sir. She doesn't know her uncle, except superficially. She doesn't trust him. She thinks Alexander is a highly suspicious character, although that wouldn't require any great acumen on anyone's part. She knows nothing about his businesses. She's never traveled with him. Her father, whom she obviously dotes on and has the highest respect for, thinks Andropulous is a highly suspicious character—the two haven't spoken for years. She's convinced that her father knows a great deal about her uncle and his businesses, but Dad refuses to discuss any aspect of the matter."

"Sounds as if we could do with Dad aboard right now," Hawkins said. "I have the feeling we could learn some very interesting things from him."

"I'm sure we could, sir. One odd thing—she's convinced that her uncle is genuinely fond of her."

Hawkins smiled. "I think it would be rather difficult not to be fond of the young lady. However, I would point out in passing, and apropos of nothing, that mass murderers have been known to dote on tiny tots."

"I hardly think he's a mass murderer, sir."

"And she's certainly not a tiny tot." He looked speculatively at Talbot. "A passing thought, John?"

"Yes." Talbot looked out through the window for an unseeing moment, then back at Hawkins. "How do we know he's not a mass murderer?"

The speculation was still in Hawkins's eyes. "You don't normally make remarks like that. Not without good reason. You have something in mind?"

"I think I have. But it's so far back in my mind

that I can't reach it. It'll come." He turned as Denholm entered the cabin. "Yes?"

"I've been with Mr. Andropulous and his friends. They have relaxed a bit. They have apparently agreed that I'm simpleminded. They are quite certain I don't know a word of Greek, but even so, they're still very cautious. Much given to allusions and cryptic references, all made, for good measure, in a Macedonian dialect."

"Which you learned at your mother's knee?"

"A bit later than that. But I'm at home in it. I don't know whether you will consider this good news or bad, sir, but Andropulous knows there are hydrogen bombs aboard that bomber. He even knows there are fifteen of them."

There was a fairly lengthy silence while the other three men in the cabin considered the implications of Denholm's words, then Hawkins said, "Good news and bad news. Good news for us, bad news for Andropulous. Well done, my boy. Very well done."

"I echo that, sir," Talbot said. "Lieutenant Denholm is miscast as either a classicist or an electronics officer. M15 should have him. There is no way that Andropulous could have learned aboard the *Ariadne* of the existence of those bombs. So he knew before. Proof, if that were needed, of our conviction that Andropulous has penetrated the Pentagon."

"I would point out, sir," Denholm said, "that the words 'hydrogen bombs' weren't actually used. Also, it's only my word against theirs."

"That's irrelevant and this is no court of law. There will be no confrontation. All that matters is that we know and they don't know that we do."

"My usefulness is over? Or do I continue to lurk?"

"Of course. The three A's must be making some contingency plans. We know now why they wanted to get aboard the *Ariadne*. What we don't now is what they intend to do now that they are here. Resume your wassailing."

"Wassailing?" Denholm sounded bitter. "I have an arrangement with Jenkins whereby I consume copious quantities of tonic water, lemon and ice. Ghastly." He turned to go but Talbot stopped him as a seaman entered and handed over a sheet of paper.

"You might as well hear what's in this." He studied the paper briefly. "This is in reply to a request we made of Greek Intelligence for as exhaustive a list as they could supply of all places where Andropulous is known either to do business or to have contacts. No names, no addresses, just towns. Forty or fifty of them. This list wasn't compiled on the spur of the moment. Greek Intelligence must have been taking a more than passing interest in the activities of our friend Andropulous over a long period—years, I would think. I wonder why. About half of those places are marked by asterisks. Again I wonder why. Was that for their own information or is it intended to suggest something to us?"

He handed the paper to Hawkins, who studied

it for a moment then said, "I know those places marked with an asterisk. I don't see their relevance in our circumstances. I can't even remotely associate them with our problem. I'd swear that none of those places have any connection with hydrogen bombs."

"So would I," Talbot said. "Maybe they handle something else. In spite of the situation we find ourselves in, maybe hydrogen bombs aren't the biggest cause for concern. If you can imagine anything worse than our present situation, that is. Could I have that back, sir?"

He sat at the desk, made some marks on the paper before him then looked up.

"Bangkok, Islamabad, Kabul, Bogotá, Miami, Mexico City, Tijuana, San Diego, Bahamas, Ocho Rios, Ankara, Sofia—Andropulous playing both sides of the fence with those last two; the ethnic Turks are having a very bad time in Bulgaria just now, but Andropulous wouldn't let that interfere with his business interests—and Amsterdam. What does that list suggest?"

"Drugs," Van Gelder said.

"Drugs. Heroin, cocaine, marijuana, you name it. Now some more towns. Tehran, Baghdad—Andropolous again playing both sides of the fence; Iran and Iraq have been at war for six years now—Tripoli, Damascus, Beirut, Athens, Rome, East Berlin, New York and London. That suggests something."

"Yes." It was Van Gelder again. "Terrorism. I'm

not quite sure why New York and London qualify."

"I seem to remember there have been two attempts, one at John F. Kennedy, the other at Heathrow, to smuggle bombs aboard planes. Both bungled, both failed. I think it's fairly safe to assume—in fact, it would be criminally negligent not to assume—that the terrorists who planned those crimes are still in residence in London and New York, waiting. Jimmy, would you please go to your cabin and bring Theodore here with whatever further results his cryptology has turned up."

Hawkins said, "I most sincerely hope that you are not thinking what you are, if you follow me."

"It may be, sir, that I am thinking what you are, if *you* follow *me*."

"What you are suggesting is that this Andropulous is some kind of mastermind—possible world coordinator—of drug smuggling? Is that what you meant by your remark that we didn't know he wasn't a mass murderer?"

"Yes, sir. What else can that list of contacts he has in drug areas mean? Where else has he accumulated his vast wealth? And we haven't added it all up yet, not by any means."

"There's no actual proof."

"All depends what you call proof. It's very powerful suggestive evidence. How far are you prepared to stretch the long arm of coincidence? To infinity?"

"And you're further suggesting he's engaged in terrorism? That he's using his vast profits from drug smuggling to finance his terrorist activities?"

"It's possible, but I don't think so. I think the two activities are being run in tandem."

"A drug peddler is one thing. A terrorist quite another. Incompatibles. Poles apart. Never the twain shall meet."

"One hesitates to contradict a senior officer. But I'm afraid you're wrong, sir. Vincent, would you enlighten the admiral? You know what I'm talking about."

"All too well, sir. October 1984, Admiral, our last submarine patrol. North Atlantic, about two hundred miles west of the Irish coast. I can remember it as if it were yesterday. We were asked to move into position to observe, but not to intercept, a small American ship en route from the States to Ireland and given its course and estimated time when it would pass a certain point. Neither the crew of this vessel nor its captain, a certain Captain Robert Anderson, who, I believe, is still at large, knew that they had been monitored from the moment they had left port by an American spy-in-the-sky satellite. We upped periscope, identified it, then downed periscope. They never saw us. It was a New England trawler, the *Valhalla*, based in Gloucester, Massachusetts, from which it had sailed a few days earlier. It transferred its cargo to an Irish tug, the *Marita Ann*, which was duly seized by the Irish Navy.

"The cargo consisted entirely of military hardware—rifles, machine guns, shotguns, pistols, hand grenades, rockets and, as I recall, about seventy thousand rounds of ammunition, all destined for the IRA. It was to have been the IRA's biggest gunrunning plot ever, but it was foiled because of what was called Operation Leprechaun, in which the CIA, our M15 and Irish Intelligence took a healthy—or unhealthy; it all depends on your point of view—interest in the activities of Noraid, an Irish-American group that specialized—for all I know it may still be specializing—in buying American arms and shipping them to the IRA in Ireland.

"Round about the same time a Panamanian-registered cargo ship by the name of *Ramsland*, chartered by the same gang who had organized the *Valhalla*, put into Boston harbor and was promptly seized by the United States Coast Guard. The *Ramsland* had secret compartments belowdecks but the Coast Guard knew all about those secret compartments. They held no less than thirty tons of marijuana, another smuggling record. The proceeds from the sale of those drugs were, of course, intended to fund IRA terrorist activities."

"We became quite interested in the drugs-terrorist connection," Talbot said, "and made some discreet inquiries. At least five other drug-terrorist connections had been discovered and broken up. It is believed that considerably more connections have not been discovered. Why should Andropulous be an exception to what appears to be a fairly well-established rule?"

"A suitably chastened admiral sits before you," Hawkins said. "We live, we learn. You two should join Denholm and offer your services to M15."

As Hawkins finished Denholm entered the cabin with Theodore, who handed over to Talbot some papers he had with him. Talbot looked at them and handed them over to Hawkins.

"Well, well, well," Hawkins said. "What an interesting coincidence or, in view of what I've just been learning, perhaps not all that much of a coincidence. Fifteen of the towns that Greek Intelligence asterisked—if that's the word—on their list. Only, in this case they give names and addresses. Isn't that splendid? Captain, a thought has occurred to me. There's one of those towns marked with an asterisk that you omitted to mention. Washington, D.C. Does that come under D for drugs or T for terrorism?"

"Neither. B for bribery. Are you about through this list, Theodore?"

"Two-thirds, I would say."

"And that will be the end of it?"

"No, Captain. There's still a last list."

"It would be gratifying if it held some more revelations, but perhaps that would be too much to hope for. How long have you been up and around, Theodore?"

"Three o'clock this morning. Three-thirty. I'm not sure, I was a bit fuzzy. If I had known what would be required of me this morning I wouldn't have gone to that birthday celebration last night."

"And it's now noon, or thereabouts. Seven

hours of beating your brains out when you weren't feeling all that hot to begin with. You must be exhausted. But I would appreciate it if you could at least finish this present list off. After that, Jimmy, I suggest that Theodore should have a drink, snack and snooze in that order." The two men left. "If you agree, Admiral, I suggest that Vincent contact Greek Intelligence after Theodore has finished that list and furnish them with a list of the towns together with the appropriate names and addresses. Could help."

"And what do you imagine Greek Intelligence can do?"

"Very little, I imagine. But they can forward the list, with utmost urgency, to Interpol. Admittedly, Interpol's writ doesn't run worldwide—they would have no clout in places like Tripoli, Tehran or Beirut—and they are an information gathering and dispensing agency not an executive unit, but they know more about bad people than any other group in the world. And ask them if they suspect —suspect, not prove—that Andropulous is engaged in drug running."

"Done, sir. Sign it 'Admiral Hawkins'?"

"Naturally."

Hawkins shook his head. "Admiral Hawkins here, Admiral Hawkins there, it seems he's signing his name everywhere. Or rather, somebody's signing it for him. I shall have to look to my checkbooks."

7

The heavy steel derrick projected upward and outward from the midships side of the *Kilcharran* at an angle about thirty degrees off the vertical. From the winch at the foot of the derrick the hawser rose upward through the pulley at the top of the derrick and then descended vertically into the sea. The lower end of the hawser was attached to a heavy metal ring which was distanced about twenty feet above the fuselage of the sunken plane; from the ring, two shorter cables, drawn taut, were attached to the two lifting slings that had been attached fore and aft to the nose and tail of the bomber.

The winch turned with what seemed to most watchers an agonizing and frustrating slowness. There was ample electrical power available to have revolved the drum several times as quickly but Captain Montgomery was in no hurry. Standing there by the winch, he exhibited about as much anxiety and tension as a man sitting with his eyes closed in a garden deck chair on a summer's afternoon. Although it was difficult to visualize, it was possible for a sling to loosen and slip and Montgomery preferred not to think what might happen if the plane should slip and strike heavily against the bottom, so he just stood patiently there, personally guiding the winch's control wheel while he listened with clamped earphones to the two divers who were accompanying the plane on its ten-foot-a-minute ascent.

After about five minutes the grotesque shape of the plane—grotesque because of the missing left wing—could be dimly discerned through the now slightly wind-ruffled surface of the sea. Another three minutes and the lifting ring came clear of the water. Montgomery centered the winch wheel, applied the brake, went to the gunwale, looked over the rail and turned to the officer by his side.

"Too close in. Fuselage is going to snag on the underside. Have to distance it a bit. More fenders fore and aft"—the side of the *Kilcharran* was already festooned with rubberized fenders—"and lay out ropes to secure the nose and tail of the plane." He returned to the winch, eased forward on a lever and slowly lowered the derrick until it was projecting outward from the ship's side at an angle of forty degrees above the horizontal. The plane, which could now be clearly seen only twenty feet below the surface, moved sluggishly outward from the ship's side. Montgomery started up the winch again and soon the top of the plane's fuselage broke the surface. He stopped the winch when the top eighteen inches was clear. The starboard wing was still beneath the surface. Montgomery turned to Admiral Hawkins.

"So far, a simple and elementary exercise. With luck, the rest of it should be equally straightforward. We cut away the appropriate section on the top of the fuselage while attaching more flotation bags to the undersides of the fuselage and the wing and inflating those. Then we'll lift a bit more until the fuselage is almost clear of the water and go inside." He lifted a ringing phone, thanked the caller and replaced the receiver. "Well, perhaps not quite so straightforward. It would appear that the timing device has stopped ticking."

"Has it now?" Hawkins didn't look particularly concerned and certainly not upset. "It could have happened at a better time and a better place. But it had to happen. So our friend is armed."

"Indeed. Still, no reason why we shouldn't go ahead as planned."

"Especially as we have no option. Warn every person on both ships. No mechanical devices to be used, no banging or crashing, everyone on tiptoes. They already know that. But I imagine they'll now redouble their caution."

A gangway had been lowered down the ship's

side until one of its feet rested on the plane's fuselage. Carrington and Grant descended and ran a tape measure back along the top of the fuselage from the cockpit—the internal distance from the cockpit to the exact location of the bomb had already been measured—to the corresponding area above. This they mopped dry with engine-room waste and then proceeded to paint the outline of a black rectangle to guide the two men with the oxyacetylene cutters who were already standing by.

Hawkins said, "How long will this take?"

"I can only guess," Montgomery said. "An hour, maybe a bit longer. We don't know how thick the fuselage skin is or how tough it is. We don't know how thick or tough the lateral reinforcing members are. What I do know is that we're going to cut with the lowest possible flame that will do the job. Even with that reduced power we're going to generate a fair amount of heat in the airspace and water below. It goes without saying that no one has ever done this sort of thing before."

"Will your standing here, supervising operations—just looking on, rather—help things along? Resolve the unknown, I mean."

"Not a bit of it. Lunch?"

"Whether we're here or in the wardroom of the *Ariadne*, it's not going to make all that much difference if this lot goes up."

"True, true. A millisecond here, a millisecond

there. The condemned man ate a hearty breakfast. In our case, lunch."

Lunch, while hardly festive, was by no means
the doom-laden affair it could have been in view
of the fact that most of the people at the table
were well aware that they were sitting on top of a
time bomb that had now ceased to tick. Conversation flowed freely but in no way resembled the
compulsive nervous chatter of those conscious of
being under stress. Professor Wotherspoon spoke
freely and often on any subject that arose, not
through garrulity but because he was a born con-
versationalist who loved discussion and the free
exchange of ideas. Andropulous, too, was far from
silent, although he appeared to have only one idea
in mind, and that was the mystery of the bomber
that had just been raised from the depths. He
had not been invited aboard the *Kilcharran* but
had seen well enough from the *Ariadne* what had
been going on. He appeared to be deeply and understandably interested in what had happened
and was going to happen to the bomber but was
clever enough not to ask any penetrating questions or say anything to indicate that he knew
anything whatever about what was going on.
Across the table Talbot caught the eye of Admiral
Hawkins, who nodded almost imperceptibly. It
was clear that they couldn't keep him completely
and totally in the dark.

"Up to now, Mr. Andropulous," Talbot said, "we
have not told you everything we know. We have

not been remiss and no apology for our silence is necessary. Our sole concern, I can assure you, was not to cause unnecessary alarm and apprehension, especially to your two young ladies. But a man like you must have a keen interest in international affairs, and you are, after all, a Greek and member of NATO and have a right to know." No one could have guessed from Talbot's openness and relaxed tone that he considered Andropulous to have a keen interest in international crime.

"The plane was an American bomber and was carrying a lethal cargo, including hydrogen and atomic bombs, almost certainly for a NATO missile base somewhere in Greece." Andropulous's expression, at first stunned, rapidly changed to grim-faced understanding. "We can only guess at what caused the crash. It could have been an engine explosion. On the other hand, it could have been carrying a variety of weapons, and one of them—obviously of the nonnuclear variety—may have malfunctioned. We don't know, we have no means of telling and probably, almost certainly, we will never know. The crew, of course, died."

Andropulous shook his head. The clear, innocent eyes were deeply tinged with sadness. "Dear God, what a tragedy, what a tragedy." He paused and considered. "But there are terrorists in this world. I know this sounds unthinkable, but could this have been a case of sabotage?"

"Impossible. This plane flew from a top-secret Air Force base where security would have been absolute. Carelessness there may have been but the idea of a deliberate implantation of any explosive device passes belief. It can only be classified as an act of God."

"I wish I shared your trust in our fellow man." Andropulous shook his head again. "There are no depths to which some inhuman monsters would not sink. But if you say it was physically impossible, then I accept that. What's past is past, I suppose, but there's also a future. What happens next, Commander?"

"Before we decide on that we'll have to wait until we get inside the plane. I understand that impacts and explosions such as those nuclear weapons have experienced can have, what shall we say, a very disturbing effect on their delicate firing-control systems."

"You—or some members of your crew—have the expertise to pass judgment on such matters?"

"Neither I nor my crew know anything about such matters. But seated only two chairs away from you is a man who does. Dr. Wickram—I will not spare his blushes—is a world-famous nuclear physicist who specializes in nuclear weaponry. We are fortunate indeed to have him aboard."

"My word, that is convenient." Andropulous leaned forward and half bowed to Wickram. "I was, of course, unaware that you were an expert on those matters. I hope you can help resolve this dreadful dilemma."

"Hardly in the dreadful category yet, Mr. Andropulous," Talbot said. "A problem, shall we say."

He turned as Denholm, who had not joined them for lunch, entered the wardroom. "Lieutenant?"

"Sorry to disturb you, sir. Lieutenant McCafferty's apologies, but would you be kind enough to come to the engine room."

Once outside, Talbot said, "What's the trouble in the engine room, Jimmy?"

"Nothing. A message from the Pentagon, sir, and some interesting information turned up by Theodore."

"I thought he was resting."

"He elected not to, sir. Just as well, as I'm sure you'll agree." He produced a slip of paper. "The Washington message."

"'Krytron device en route direct New York–Athens via Concorde.' My word, someone over there does carry some clout. I detect the hand of the President in this. Can't you just see the outrage of a hundred-odd Europe-bound passengers when they find themselves being dumped on the tarmac of John F. Kennedy in favor of a teeny-weeny electrical device? Not that they'll know why they have been dumped. It goes on: 'Fullest cooperation British Airways, Spanish and Italian authorities.'"

"Why Spain and Italy?" Denholm said. "You don't require permission to overfly friendly countries. Just Air Control notification, that's all."

"Except, I imagine when you're going to upset their normal peace and quiet with a nonstop sonic boom. Message ends: 'ETA your time 3 P.M.' Just over an hour. We'll have to make arrangements to have a plane standing by in the Athens airport. Let's see what Theodore has for us. Something of significance, I imagine."

Theodore had, indeed, found something of significance, although its relevance was not immediately evident.

"I've started on the third and last list, Captain," Theodore said, "and this is the sixth name I've come up with. George Skepertzis. Full Washington address. Under the address, as you see, it says Ref. K.K., T.T. Means nothing to me."

"Nor to me," Talbot said. "Anything to you, Lieutenant?"

"It might. Skepertzis is a Greek name, that's sure. Could be a fellow countryman of Andropulous. And if our friend has contacts in the Pentagon, you can lay odds that he wouldn't be writing them, using their names, care of the Pentagon. You'd expect Andropulous to use a buffer man, a go-between."

"You're probably right. So a message to the bank asking if they have any accounts under those initials and one to the FBI to find out if there are any Air Force generals or admirals with those initials. A shot in the dark, of course, but it might find a target. In the remote event of their contemplating a sound night's sleep, a personal message to the President, via the FBI, that the tick...tick...tick has stopped and that the atomic mine is armed. We'll clear it with the admiral first. Would you ask him to join us. Have Number One and Dr. Wickram come along, too. I suggest the bridge. I'm sure you'll think up a suitable excuse on the way to the wardroom."

"I don't have to think, sir. It's second nature now."

"Fair enough." Hawkins laid down the three radio messages that Talbot had already drafted. "The Greek Ministry of Defense will have a plane standing by when the Concorde lands. If its estimated time of arrival is reasonably accurate we should have this krytron device in Santorini about three-thirty. Even allowing for the fact that your men will have to row to and from at least Cape Akrotiri we should have the device aboard by five P.M. There's at least an even chance that the messages to the FBI and the Washington bank may produce some positive results. As to the news that the mine is armed, we shall await the presidential reaction with interest. Send these at once. You have some other matters on your mind, Captain. Urgent, I take it?"

"As you said yourself not so long ago, sir, time *is* on the wing. Questions, sir, and we'd better try to find some answers quickly. Why was Andropulous so restrained in his questioning about the bomber? Because—apart from that ticking time device—he already knew everything there was to know and saw no point in asking questions when he already held the answers.

"Why did he express no surprise at Dr. Wickram here just happening to be aboard at this critical juncture? Even the most innocent of people would have thought it the most extraordinary coincidence that Dr. Wickram should be here at the moment when he was most needed and would have said so.

"What's going to pass through that crafty and calculating mind when he sees us hauling that atom bomb out of the fuselage? And what are we going to do to satisfy his curiosity?"

"I can answer your last two questions *and* explain my presence here," Wickram said. "I've had time to think, although, to be honest, it didn't require all that much thought. You heard that the plane had hydrogen bombs aboard, you didn't know what the degree of danger was, so you called in the resident expert. That's me. The resident expert informs you there is a high degree of danger. There's no way to prevent a slow but continuous degree of radioactive emanations from a hydrogen bomb, and there are fifteen of those aboard that plane. This radioactivity builds up inside the atom bomb, which is of an entirely different construction, until the critical stage is reached. Then it's good night, all. All a question of mass, really."

"This really happens?"

"How the hell should I know? I've just invented it. But it sounds scientific enough and more than vaguely plausible. Your average citizen has a zero knowledge level of nuclear weaponry. Who is going to dream of questioning the word of a world-famous nuclear physicist, which, in case you've forgotten Commander Talbot's words, is me."

Talbot smiled. "I wouldn't dream of it, Dr. Wickram. Excellent. Next query. What are Andropulous's code lists doing aboard the *Ariadne*?"

"Well, to start with," Hawkins said, "you put them there. No need for massive restraint, Captain. You had something else in mind?"

"Wrong question. Why did he leave them behind? He forgot? Not likely. Not something as important as that. Because he thought they'd never be found? Possible, but again not likely. Because he thought that if anyone found them then it would be unlikely that that person would recognize it as a code and try to decode it? Rather more likely, but I think the real reason is that he thought it would be too dangerous to bring them aboard the *Ariadne*. The very fact that that was the only item he chose to salvage from the wreck would have been significant and suspicious in itself. So he elected to leave them behind and recover them later by diving. He may always have had this possibility in his mind and if he did he wouldn't have left them in a cardboard folder. So he chose a waterproof metal box.

"Recovery of the box from the bottom of the sea would mean the presence or availability of a diving ship. Just a hunch. I think that the *Delos* was sunk by accident and not by design. Probably Andropulous never visualized the need of a diving ship for that purpose. But a convenient diving ship would have been useful for other purposes, such as, dare I suggest, the recovery of nuclear weapons from a sunken bomber. They—whoever

they are—wouldn't have brought it down anywhere in the Sea of Crete—that's the area between the Peloponnese to the west, the
Dodecanese to the east, the Cyclades to the north
and Crete to the south—because by far the
greater part of that area is between fifteen
hundred and seven thousand feet—much too
deep for recovery by diving. Maybe it was meant
to bring it down where it was brought down.
Maybe this hypothetical diving ship was meant to
be where we inconveniently were."

"It's a long shot," Hawkins said, "but no stone
unturned, is that it? What you would like to know
is whether there is any diving ship based in those
parts or temporarily located or cruising by." Talbot
nodded. "Finding out is no problem."

"Heraklion in Crete?"

"Of course. The U.S. Air Force base there is
our main center for electronic surveillance in
those parts. They use AWACs and other high-
flying radar planes to monitor Soviet, Libyan and
other countries' military movements. The Greek
Air Force uses their Phantoms and Mirages for
the same purpose. I know the base commander
rather well. An immediate signal. They'll either
find out in very short order or have the information ready. A couple of hours should do it."

"I speak in no spirit of complaint," Captain
Montgomery said to Talbot. His voice, in fact,
held a marked note of complaint. "But I think we
might have been spared this." He indicated a

bank of heavy dark cloud approaching from the northwest. "The wind's already Force 5 and we're beginning to rock a bit. Travel agents wouldn't like this at all. This is supposed to be a golden summer's day in the golden Aegean."

"Force 5 isn't uncommon here in the afternoons, even at this time of year. Rain *is* most unusual but it looks as if we're going to have quite a lot of the unusual in the very near future. Weather forecast is poor and the barometer unhappy." Talbot looked over the rail of the *Kilcharran*. "And this is what makes you unhappy."

Montgomery's ship was not, in fact, rocking at all. Headed directly northwest into the gentle three-foot swell, it was quite motionless, which couldn't be said for the plane lashed alongside. Because of its much shorter length and the fact that it was nine-tenths submerged, it was reacting quite badly to the swell, pitching rather noticeably to and fro and snubbing alternately on the ropes that secured its nose and the remnants of its tail to the *Kilcharran*. Cutting the metal and maintaining balance was becoming increasingly difficult for the oxyacetylene team on top of the fuselage as the tops of the swells periodically washed over the area on which they were working. They had already reached the stage where they were spending more time looking after their own safety than using their torches.

"Not so much unhappy as annoyed. Their rate of progress has been reduced to almost zero and God knows they were moving slowly enough even in good conditions—that fuselage and especially the transverse members are proving much tougher than expected. If things don't improve— and looking at that weather coming at us, I'm sure they won't—I'm going to have to withdraw the cutters. They're in no danger, of course, but the plane might very well be. We have no way of knowing how weakened the nose or tail may be and I don't care to imagine what will happen if one of them comes off."

"So you're going to float it astern on a single towrope?"

"I don't see that I have any option. I'll build a cradle of ropes round the nose and wing of the plane, attach to it a single rope—a heavy one, to act as a spring—and let it drift a cable length astern. Have to inform the admiral first."

"No need. He never interferes with an expert. An unpleasant thought occurs, Captain. What happens if it breaks loose?"

"Send a boat out—rowing, of course—to secure it with an anchor."

"And if that goes?"

"We puncture the flotation bags and sink it. Can't have it drifting all over the shop ready to blow the whole works whenever the first ship's engines come within auditory range."

"And if it sinks where it is, we, of course, won't be able to move from here."

"You can't have everything."

* * *

"Agreed," Hawkins said. "Montgomery's got no option. When is he starting?"

"Any moment. Perhaps you might have a word with him. I said that there was no question but that you would agree, but I think he'd like your say-so."

"Of course," Hawkins said. "What's your weather forecast?"

"Deteriorating. Any word from the Washington Bank, the FBI or Heraklion?"

"Nothing. Just a lot of unsolicited rubbish from diverse heads of state, presidents, premiers and so forth commiserating with us in one breath and asking us why we aren't doing something about it in the second breath. One wonders how the news has been leaked."

"I don't know, sir. What's more, I really don't care."

"Nor I." He waved to some papers on his desk. "Want to read them? They don't know that the tick . . . tick . . . tick has stopped."

"I don't want to read them."

"I didn't think you would. What's next for you, John?"

"I didn't have much sleep last night. It's quite possible I may lack some tonight. Now's the time. Nothing I can do."

"An excellent idea. Same for me when I come back from the *Kilcharran*."

When Talbot emerged from his day cabin and

passed through the bridge shortly after six o'clock in the evening it should still have been broad daylight, but so low was the level of light in the sky that it could well have been late twilight. He found Van Gelder and Denholm waiting for him.

"We have not been idle," Van Gelder said. "Neither has Captain Montgomery. He's got the bomber strung out about a cable length to the southeast. Riding quite badly—it's either a Force 6 or 7 out there—but it seems to be holding together. He's got a searchlight—well, a six-inch signaling lamp—on it, either to check that it doesn't break away or to discourage the disaffected from snaffling it, although why there should be anyone around, or daft enough, to try that I can't imagine. I'd advise against going out on the wing to have a look, sir. You might get washed away." The rain falling from the black and leaden skies was of the torrential or tropical-downpour variety, the heavy warm drops rebounding six inches from the deck.

"I take your point." He looked at the brown metal box lying on the deck. "What's That?"

"*Voilà!*" Denholm seized the handle set into the top and swept off the cover with all the panache of a stage magician unveiling his latest impossible trick. "The pièce de résistance." What was presumably the control panel on the top of the box was singularly unimpressive and old-fashioned, reminiscent of a prewar radio, with two calibrated dials, some knobs, a press button and two orange hemispherical glass domes let into the surface.

"The krytron, I assume," Talbot said.

"No less. Three cheers for presidents. This particular one has been as good as his word."

"Excellent. Really excellent. Let's only hope we get the chance to use it under, let us say, optimal circumstances."

"'Optimal' is the word," Denholm said. "Very simple device—as far as operating is concerned, that is. Inside, it's probably fiendishly complicated. This particular model—there may be others—runs off a twenty-four-volt battery." He placed his forefinger on a button. "I depress this —and hey, presto!"

"If you're trying to make me nervous, Jimmy, you're succeeding. Take your finger off that damned button."

Denholm depressed it several times. "No battery. We supply that. No problem. And under those two orange domes are two switches that have to be rotated through a hundred eighty degrees. Specially designed, you see, for careless clowns like me. As an added precaution, you can't unscrew those domes. One sharp tap with a light metal object, the instructions say, and they disintegrate. Again, I should imagine, designed with people like me in mind, in case we remove the tops and start twiddling the switches around. Designed, if you follow me, to be a one-time operation. The only time those switches will ever be exposed is immediately before the firing button is depressed."

"When are you going to attach the battery?"

"As an added precaution—this is *my* precaution—only immediately before use. These are positive and negative connections. We use spring-loaded crocodile clips. Two seconds to attach the clips. Three seconds to crack the domes and align the switches. One second to press the button. Nothing could be simpler. Only one other trifling requirement, sir—that we have that atom bomb, on its own and a long, long way from anywhere and us at a very prudent distance when we detonate it."

"You ask for very little, Jimmy." Talbot looked out at the driving rain and the dark and now whitecapped seas. "We may have to wait a little—an hour or two as an optimistic guess, all night as a pessimistic one—before we can even begin to move. Anything else?"

"I repeat, we have not been idle," Van Gelder said. "We've heard from the Heraklion air base. "There is—or was—a diving vessel in the near vicinity, if you can call the western tip of Crete the near vicinity."

"Is—or was?"

"Was. It was anchored off Suda Bay for a couple of days and apparently took off about one o'clock this morning. As you know, Suda Bay is a very hush-hush Greek naval base, and the area is very protected, very restricted. Foreign vessels, even harmless cruising yachts, are definitely not welcomed. Suda Bay naturally took an interest in this lad. It's their business to be suspicious, especially at a time when NATO are operating in the area."

"What did they find out?"

"Precious little. It was called the *Taormina* and registered in Panama."

"A Sicilian name? No significance. Panama—a convenience registry, some of the most successful oceangoing crooks in the world are registered there. Anyway, you don't have to be an artist to change both names in very short order; all you require is a couple of pots of paint and a set of stencils. Where had it come from?"

"They didn't know. As it had anchored offshore, it didn't have to register with either the customs or the port authorities. But they did know that it took off in a roughly northeasterly direction, which, just coincidentally, is the course it would have taken if it were heading for Santorini. And as Suda Bay is just under a hundred miles from here, even a slow ship could have been in this area well before the bomber came down. So your hunch could have been right, sir. Only problem is, we've seen no sign of him."

"Could have been a coincidence. Could have been that the *Delos* warned him off. Did Heraklion say anything about going to have a look for this ship?"

"No. Jimmy and I discussed the idea but we didn't think it important enough to disturb you when you were, ah, resting lightly. And the admiral."

"Probably unimportant. We should have a go.

Normally, that is. Where does Heraklion lie from here. About due south?"

"Near enough."

"A couple of planes, one carrying out a sweep to the north, the other to the east, should locate this lad, if he is in the area, in half an hour, probably less. Part of an urgent NATO exercise, you understand. But conditions aren't normal. A waste of time in near-zero visibility. An option we'll keep in mind for better weather. Anything else?"

"Yes. We've heard from both the Washington bank and the FBI. Mixed results, you might say. Under the initials, K.K., the bank says it has a certain Kyriakos Katzanevakis."

"Promising. You could hardly get anything more Grecian than that."

"Under T.T., they have a Thomas Thompson. You can't have anything more Anglo-Saxon than that. The FBI say there are no high-ranking officers in the Pentagon—by which I take it they mean admirals and Air Force generals or, at the outside, vice admirals and lieutenant generals—with those initials."

"On the face of it, disappointing, but it may equally well be just another step in the laundering cover-up, another step to distance themselves from their paymaster. The FBI haven't been in touch with the bank? Of course not. We didn't even mention the bank to them. Remiss of us. No, remiss of me. The bank must have addresses for Messrs. K.K. and T.T., and although those will most certainly turn out to be accommodation addresses, they may lead to something else. And another omission, again my fault entirely. We didn't let the FBI have the name and address of this George Skepertzis. We'll do that now. There's an outside chance that the FBI may be able to link Skepertzis, K.K. and T.T. together. And what was the presidential reaction to the stopping of the tick . . . tick . . . tick?"

"He appears to be beyond any further reaction."

Montgomery sipped his drink, gazed gloomily through his cabin window, winced and looked away.

"The weather has deteriorated in the past half hour, Commander Talbot."

"It couldn't possibly be any worse than it was half an hour ago."

"I'm an expert on such matters." Montgomery sighed. "Makes me quite homesick for the Mountains of Mourne. We get a lot of rainfall in the Mountains of Mourne. Do you see this lot clearing up in the near future?"

"Not this side of midnight."

"And that would be an optimistic estimate, I'm thinking. By the time we haul this damn bomber back alongside, cut away the hole in the fuselage, hoist it out of the water and extract the bomb, it'll be dawn. At least. Might possibly be well into the morning. You'll understand if I turn down your offer to join you for dinner. An early snack for me, then bed. Might have to get up anytime during the night. I'll have a couple of boys on the poop all night, watching the plane and with orders to wake me as soon as they think the weather has moderated enough for us to start hauling it in."

Dr. Wickram said, "How's that for a brief résumé of the speech I shall so reluctantly make at the table tonight. Not too much, I would have thought, and not too little?"

"Perfect. Perhaps the tone a thought more doomladen?"

"A half octave deeper, you think? Odd, isn't it, how easily this mendacity comes to one?"

"Aboard the *Ariadne*, it's become positively endemic. Very catching."

"I've just had a word with Eugenia," Denholm said. "I thought you ought to know."

"You spoke to her privately, I take it?"

"Yes, sir. In her cabin. Number One's cabin, that is to say."

"You surprise me, Jimmy."

"If I may say so, sir, with some dignity, we had been discussing matters on a purely intellectual level. Very bright girl. Going for a double first at the university. Language and literature, Greek ancient and modern."

"Ah! Deep calling unto deep."

"I wouldn't call it that, because I spoke only in English. I was under the impression that she was convinced that I didn't speak a word of Greek."

"She's no longer convinced? A close observer, the young lady? Perhaps you registered a flicker of expression when something was said in Greek when you should have registered nothing. I suspect you were trapped in your innocent youth by some fiendish feminine wile."

"How would you react, sir, if you were told that a scorpion was crawling up your shoe."

Talbot smiled. "She spoke in Greek, of course. You immediately carried out a hurried check to locate this loathsome monster. Anybody would have fallen for it. You have not suffered too much chagrin and mortification, I hope?"

"Not really, sir. She's too nice. And too worried. Wanted to confide in me."

"Alas, the days when lovely young ladies wanted to confide in me appear to be over."

"I think she's a little scared of you, sir. So is Irene. She wanted to talk about Andropulous. Girls talk, of course, and I suppose there's really no one else on the ship they can talk to. That's not quite fair, I suppose, they're clearly very close friends. Seems that Irene repeated to her, more or less verbatim, the conversation she had with Number One this morning and told her she'd told Vincent everything she knew about her Uncle Adam. It would appear that Eugenia knows something about Uncle Adam that his niece doesn't know. May I have a drink, sir? I've been awash since dawn in tonic and lemon."

"Help yourself. Revelations, is that it?"

"I don't know how you'd classify it, sir, but I

know you'll find it very interesting. Eugenia's father has quite a lot in common with Irene's father—apparently they're good friends—they're both wealthy businessmen, they both know Andropulous and both think he's a crook. Well, nothing new in that so far. We all think he's a crook. But Eugenia's father, unlike Irene's, is willing to talk freely and at length about Andropulous and Eugenia hasn't talked about it to Irene, because she doesn't wish to hurt her feelings." Denholm sampled his drink and sighed in satisfaction. "It would seem that Adamantios Spyros Andropulous has a pathological hatred of Americans."

"Well, we know he's intelligent, so he had to have a reason.

"He had. Two. His son and only nephew. Apparently, he doted on them. Eugenia quite believes this, because she says that Andropulous is unquestionably fond of Irene and herself. A feeling that they don't reciprocate."

"What about his son and nephew?"

"Disappeared in most mysterious circumstances. Never to be seen again. Andropulous is convinced that they were done in by the American CIA."

"The CIA have a reputation, justified or not, for eliminating people they regard as undesirables. But they usually have a reason, again whether that is justifiable or not. Does Eugenia's old man know the reason?"

"Yes. He says—and he's convince of this—that the two young men were heroin peddlers."

"Well, well. Ties in all too well with what we have been increasingly suspecting. There are times, Jimmy, when I regard the CIA as being a much maligned lot."

The atmosphere at the dinner table that night was noticeably less relaxed than it had been at lunchtime. Conversation flowed less freely than it had then, and three men in particular, Hawkins, Talbot and Van Gelder, seemed more given to brief and introspective silences, occasionally gazing at some object or objects that lay beyond a distant horizon. There was nothing that one could put a finger on and the insensitive would have failed to recognize that there was anything amiss. Andropulous proved that he was not one of those.

"I do not wish to pry, gentlemen, and I may be quite wrong, I frequently am, but do I not detect a certain aura of uneasiness, even of tension at the table tonight?" His smile was as open and ingenuous as his words had been frank and candid. "Or is it my imagination? You are surprised, perhaps, Commander Talbot?"

"No, not really." The only thing that surprised Talbot was that Andropulous had taken so long in getting around to it. "You are very perceptive, Mr. Andropulous. I'm rather disappointed, I must say. I thought—or hoped—that our concern was better concealed than that."

"Concern, Captain?"

"To a slight degree only. No real anxiety yet. No reason in the world why you shouldn't know as much as we do." As Dr. Wickram had said, Talbot reflected, lying required little practice to become second nature. There was every reason in the world why Andropulous should not know as much as he did. "You know, of course, that the bad weather has forced us to suspend operations on the bomber?"

"I have seen that it is riding several hundred meters astern of us. Operations? What operations, Captain? You are trying to recover those wicked weapons?"

"Just one of them. An atom bomb."

"Why only one?"

"Dr. Wickram? Would you kindly explain?"

"Certainly. Well, as far as I can. What we have here is a situation of considerable complexity and doubt, because we are dealing largely with the unknown. You will be aware that a nuclear explosion occurs when a critical mass of uranium or plutonium is reached. Now, there's no way to prevent a slow but continuous degree of radioactive emanations from a hydrogen bomb, and there are fifteen of them aboard that plane. This radioactivity builds up inside the atom bomb, which is of an entirely different construction, until the critical mass of the atom bomb is reached. Then the atom bomb goes poof! Unfortunately, because of something we call sympathetic detonation, the hydrogen bombs also go poof! I will not dwell on what will happen to us.

"Normally, because of this well-known danger, hydrogen bombs and atom bombs are never stored together, not, at least, for any period of time. Twenty-four hours is regarded as a safe period, and a plane, as in this instance, can easily make a long-distance flight with them together, at the end of which, of course, they would immediately be stored separately. What happens after twenty-four hours, we simply don't know, although some of us—I am one—believe that the situation deteriorates very rapidly thereafter.

"Incidentally, that's why I have asked the captain to stop all engines and generators. It is an established fact that acoustical vibrations hasten the onset of the critical period."

Wickram's deep, solemn and authoritative voice carried absolute conviction. Had he not known, Talbot thought, that Dr. Wickram was talking scientific malarkey, he, for one, would have believed every word he said.

"So you will readily appreciate that it is of the utmost urgency that we remove that atom bomb from the plane as soon as possible and then take it away—by sail, of course, that's why the *Angelina* is alongside; the critical mass will decay only very slowly—to some distant spot. Some very distant spot. There we will deposit it gently on the ocean floor."

"How will you do that?" Andropulous said. "Deposit it gently, I mean. The ocean could be thousands of feet deep at the spot. Wouldn't the bomb accelerate all the way down?"

Wickram smiled tolerantly. "I have discussed the matter with Captain Montgomery of the *Kil-*

charran." He had not, in fact, discussed the matter with anybody. "We attach a flotation bag to the bomb, inflate it until it achieves a very slight negative buoyancy, and then it will float down like a feather to the ocean floor."

"And then?"

"And then nothing." If Wickram were having visions of a passenger cruise liner passing over an armed atomic mine, he kept his visions to himself. "It will decay and corrode slowly over the years, perhaps even over the centuries. May give rise to a few digestive upsets for some passing fish. I don't know. What I do know is that if we don't get rid of that damned beast with all dispatch we're going to suffer more than a few digestive problems. Better that some of us—those concerned with the recovery of the bomb—have a sleepless night than that we all sleep forever."

8

Talbot stirred, half sat up in his bunk and blinked at the overhead light that had suddenly come on in his day cabin. Van Gelder was standing in the doorway.

"Two-thirty. An ungodly hour, Vincent. Something is afoot. Weather moderated and Captain Montgomery hauling in the plane?"

"Yes, sir. But there's something more immediately urgent. Jenkins is missing."

Talbot swung his feet to the deck. "Jenkins? I won't say 'missing' or 'how can he be missing?' If you say he is, he is. You've had a search carried out of course?"

"Of course. Forty volunteers. You know how popular Jenkins is." Talbot knew. Jenkins, their mess steward and a Marine of fifteen years' standing, a man whose calmness, efficiency and resource were matched ony by his sense of humor, was highly regarded by everyone who knew him.

"Can Brown cast any light on this?" Marine Sergeant Brown, a man as rockline and solid as Chief McKenzie, was Jenkins's closest friend on the ship. Both men were in the habit of having a tipple in the pantry when the day's work was done, an illicit practice which Talbot tacitly and readily condoned. Their tipple invariably stopped at that, just one; even in the elite Royal Marines it would have been difficult to find two men like them.

"Nothing, sir. They went down to their mess together. Brown turned in while Jenkins started on a letter to his wife. That was the last Brown saw of him."

"Who discovered his absence?"

"Carter. The master-at-arms. You know how he likes to prowl around at odd hours of the day and night looking for nonexistent crime. He went up to the wardroom and pantry, found nothing, returned to the Marine mess deck and woke Brown. They carried out a brief search. Again nothing. Then they came to me."

"It would be pointless to ask you if you have any ideas?"

"Pointless. Brown seems convinced he's no longer aboard the ship. He says that Jenkins never sleep-walked, drank only sparingly and was devoted to his wife and two daughters. He had no

problems—Brown is certain of that—and no enemies aboard the ship. Well, among the crew, that
is. Brown is further convinced that Jenkins stumbled across something he shouldn't have or saw
something he shouldn't have seen, although how
he could do anything like that while sitting in the
mess writing to his wife is difficult to imagine.
His suspicions immediately centered on Andropulous and company—I gather he and Jenkins
have talked quite a lot about them—he was all for
going down to Andropulous's cabin and beating
the living daylights out of him. I had some difficulty in restraining him, although privately, I
must say, I found it rather an appealing prospect."

"An understandable reaction on his part." He
paused. "I can't see how Andropulous or his
friends could have any possible connection with
this or have any conceivable reason for knocking
him off. Do you think there's a remote chance
that he might have gone aboard the *Kilcharran*?"

"No earthly reason why he should have but the
thought did occur. I asked Danforth—he's the
Kilcharran's chief officer—if he'd have a look
around, so he collected some of his crew and carried out a search. There aren't many places you
can hide—or be hidden—on a diving ship. Took
them less than ten minutes to be sure he wasn't
anywhere aboard."

"Nothing we can do at the moment. I have the
uncomfortable feeling that there's nothing we're
going to be able to do either. Let's go and see how
Captain Montgomery is getting on."

The wind had dropped to Force 3, the sea was no more than choppy and the rain had eased, but only slightly, from torrential to heavy. Montgomery, clad in streaming oilskins, was at the winch: the plane, still bobbing rather uncomfortably, was slowly but steadily nearing the stern of the diving ship. The oxyacetylene crew, also in oilskins, were standing by the guardrail, torches at the ready.

Talbot said, "Your men are going to be able to maintain their footing?"

"It won't be easy. The plane should steady up a bit when we secure it fore and aft and we'll have ropes on the men, of course. And this confounded rain doesn't help. I think we should be able to make some progress but it'll be slow. Point is, this may be as good weather as we're going to get. No point in your remaining, Commander, you'd be better off in your bunk. I'll let you know when we've cut away the section and are ready to lift." He wiped rain away from his eyes. "I hear you've lost your chief steward. Bloody odd, isn't it? Do you suspect foul play?"

"I'm at the stage where I'm about ready to suspect anything or anybody. Van Gelder and I are agreed that it couldn't have happened accidentally, so it must have happened on purpose and not, of course, his purpose. Yes, foul play. As to what kind of foul play and the identity of the person or persons responsible, we don't have a clue."

* * *

It should have been dawn, but it wasn't, when Van Gelder roused Talbot shortly after six-thirty in the morning. The sky was still heavy and dark, and neither the wind nor the steadily drumming rain had improved in the past four hours.

"So much for your breathless Aegean dawns," Talbot said. "I take it that Captain Montgomery has cut away that section of the plane's fuselage?"

"Forty minutes ago. He's got the fuselage more than halfway out of the water already."

"How are the winch and the derrick taking the strain?"

"Very little strain, I believe. He's secured four more flotation bags under the fuselage and wing and letting compressed air do most of the work. He asks if you'd like to come along. Oh, and we've had a communication from Greek Intelligence about Andropulous."

"You don't seem very excited about it."

"I'm not. Interesting, but doesn't really help us. It just confirms that our suspicions about Uncle Adam are far from groundless. They've passed on our messages to Interpol. It seems—the message, I must say, is couched in very guarded language —that both Greek Intelligence and Interpol have been taking a considerable interest in Andropulous for several years. Both are certain that our friend is engaged in highly illegal activities but if this was a trial in a Scottish court of law the verdict would be 'not proven.' They have no hard evidence. Andropulous acts through intermediaries who operate through other intermediaries and so on until the trail either runs cold or, occasionally, ends up in shell companies in Panama and the Bahamas, where much of his money is stashed away. The banks there consistently refuse to acknowledge letters and cables; in fact, they won't even acknowledge his existence. No cooperation from the Swiss banks either. They'll only open up their books if the depositor has been convicted of what is also regarded as a crime in Switzerland. He hasn't been convicted of anything."

"Illegal activities? What illegal activities?"

"Drugs. Message ends with a request—sounds more like a demand the way they put it—that this information be treated in total secrecy, utter and absolute confidentiality. Words to that effect."

"What information? They haven't given us any information that we didn't already suspect or have. No mention of the one item of information we'd like to know. Who, either in the government, the civil service or the top echelons in the armed forces, is Andropulous's powerful protector and friend. Possibly they don't know, more probably they don't want us to know. Nothing from Washington?"

"Not a word. Maybe the FBI don't work at night."

"More likely that other people don't work at night. It's eleven-thirty P.M. their time, the banks are shut and all the staffs to hell and gone until tomorrow morning. We may have to wait hours before we hear anything."

"We're nearly there," Captain Montgomery said. "We'll stop hoisting—in this case, more lifting from below than hoisting—when the water level drops below the floor of the cabin. That way we won't get our feet wet when we go inside."

Talbot looked over the side to where a man, torch in his hand pointing downward, sat with his legs dangling through the rectangular hole that had been cut in the fuselage.

"We're going to get a lot more than our feet wet before we get there. We've got to pass first through the compartment under the flight deck and that will still have a great deal of water in it."

"I don't understand," Montgomery said. "I mean we don't have to. We just drop down through the hole we've made in the fuselage."

"That's fine, if all we want to do is confine ourselves to the cargo hold. But you can't get into the flight deck from there. There's a heavy steel door in the bulkhead and the clamps are secured on the for'ard side. So if we want to get at those clamps you have to do it from the flight-deck side, and to do that you must pass through the flooded compartment first."

"Why should we want to open that door at all?"

"Because the clamps holding the atom bomb in place have padlocks. Where is one of the first places you'd look if you were searching for a key to the padlocks?"

"Ah! Of course. The pockets of the dead men."

"Enough, Captain," the man on the fuselage called out. "Deck's clear."

Montgomery centered the winch and applied the brake, then checked the fore and aft securing ropes. When he had them adjusted to his satisfaction he said, "Won't be long, gentlemen. Just going to have a first-hand look."

"Van Gelder and I are coming with you. We've brought our suits." He checked the level of the top of the jagged hole in the nose cone relative to the surface of the sea. "I don't think we'll be needing our helmets."

They did not, as it proved, require their helmets; the compartment under the flight deck was no more than two-thirds full. They moved along to the opened hatch and hauled themselves up into the space behind the pilot's seats. Montgomery looked at the two dead men and screwed his eyes momentarily shut.

"What a bloody awful mess. And to think that the bastard responsible is still walking around free as air."

"I don't think he will be for much longer."

"But you've said yourself you don't have the evidence to convict him."

"Andropulous will never come to trial. Vincent, would you bang open that door and show Captain Montgomery where our friend is."

"No banging. Maybe our friend doesn't like banging." Van Gelder produced a large stillson wrench. "Persuasion. Aren't you coming, sir?"

"In a moment." They left and Talbot addressed himself to the highly distasteful task of searching through the dead men's pockets. He found nothing. He searched through every shelf, locker and compartment in the cockpit. Again, nothing. He moved aft and joined Montgomery and Van Gelder.

"Nothing, sir?"

"Nothing. And nothing I can find anywhere in the flight deck."

Montgomery grimaced. "You were, of course, looking through the pockets of the dead men. Sooner you than me. This is a very big plane. The key—if there ever was a key—could have been tucked away anywhere. I don't give much for our chances of recovering it. So other methods. Your Number One suggests a corrosive to cut through those clamps. Wouldn't it be easier just to use an old-fashioned hacksaw?"

"I wouldn't recommmend it, sir," Van Gelder said. "If you were to try I'd rather be a couple of hundred miles away at the time. I don't know how intelligent this armed listening device is, but I would question whether it's clever enough to tell the difference between the rhythmic rasping of a hacksaw and the pulse of an engine."

"I agree with Vincent," Talbot said. "Even if it were only a one-in-ten-thousand chance—and for all we know it might be a one-in-one chance —the risk still isn't worth taking. Lady Luck has been riding with us so far but she might take a poor view of our pushing her too far."

"So corrosives, you think? I have my doubts."
Montgomery stopped to examine the clamps more
closely. "I should have carried out some prelimi-
nary test aboard, I suppose, but I never thought
those clamps would be so thick or made, as I suspect they are, of hardened steel. The only corrosive I have aboard is sulphuric acid. Neat
sulphuric, H_2SO_4 at specific gravity 1800—vitriol,
if you like—is a highly corrosive agent when applied to most substances, which is why it is
usually carried in glass carboys, which are immune to the corrosive action of acids. But I think
it would find this a very tough meal to digest. Pa-
tience and diligence, of course, and I'm sure it
would do the trick, but it might take hours."

Talbot said, "What do you think, Vincent?"

"I'm no expert. I should imagine Captain
Montgomery is quite correct. So no corrosives, no
hacksaws, no oxyacetylene torches." Van Gelder
hoisted the big stillson in his hand. "This."

Talbot looked at the clamps and their mount-
ings, then nodded. "Of course. That. We're not
very bright, are we? At least I'm not." He looked
at the way the clamps were secured to the side of
the fuselage and the floor: each of the bases of
the four retaining arms of the clamps were fitted
over two bolts and were held in place by heavy
inch-and-a-half nuts. "We leave the clamps in
place and free the bases instead. See how stiff
those nuts are, will you?"

Van Gelder applied the stillson to one of the

nuts, adjusted the grip and heaved. The nut was big and tightly jammed in position but a stillson wrench affords great leverage. The nut turned easily.

"Simple," Van Gelder said.

"Indeed." Talbot looked at the length of the retaining arms, which projected at ninety degrees from each other, then gauged the width of the hole that had been cut overhead. "What's not so simple is getting the bomb up through the hole. With those arms in position there's just not enough clearance for it to go through. We'll have to widen the hole. You can do that, Captain?"

"No bother. Just means that we'll have to lower the fuselage down to its previous position. I'm coming around to Van Gelder's view about taking zero chances. I want as much water as possible in this compartment to dissipate the heat of the torches. It'll take a couple of hours, maybe longer, to do the job, but better two or three hours late down here than twenty years early you know where."

Van Gelder said, "Do I undo those nuts now?"

"No. We're stable enough at the moment. But if the fuselage returns to its previous position of being almost submerged and then the weather blows up—well, I don't think it would be a very clever idea to have an armed atomic mine rolling about all over the shop."

"I don't think so either."

* * *

Talbot and Van Gelder were back aboard the *Ariadne* and having coffee in the deserted wardroom when a seaman from the radio room entered and handed Talbot a message. Talbot read it and handed it to Van Gelder, who read it twice, then looked at his captain with a certain thoughtful surprise.

"Looks as if I have been casting unjust aspersions on the FBI, sir. It further looks as if they do work at night."

"Even better, it seems as if they have no compunction about waking others, such as bank managers, in the middle of the night and making them work also. One gathers from the message that Andropulous's mysterious friend George Skepertzis does know the even more mysterious Kyriakos Katzanevakis and Thomas Thompson."

"If G.S. deposits one million dollars each in the accounts of K.K. and T.T. and has given them smaller sums on previous occasions one gathers that they are more than passing acquaintances. Unfortunately, it seems that the one person who could identify them, the bank clerk who handled the accounts of all three men, has been transferred elsewhere. They say that they are pursuing inquiries, whatever that means."

"It means, I'm certain, that the FBI are going to drag this unfortunate bank clerk from his bed and have him conduct an identity parade."

"I find it hard, somehow, to visualize generals

and admirals voluntarily consenting to line up for inspection."

"They won't have to. The FBI or the Pentagon itself is bound to have pictures of them." Talbot looked out of the window. "Dawn is definitely in the sky and the rain has eased off to no more than a drizzle. I suggest we contact the Heraklion air base and ask them if they'll kindly go and have a look for the diving ship *Taormina*."

Together with the admiral and the two scientists, Talbot and Van Gelder were just finishing breakfast when a messenger arrived from the *Kilcharran*. Captain Montgomery, he informed them, had just finished enlarging the opening on the top of the bomber's fuselage and was about to raise the plane again. Would they care to come across? He had made especial mention of Lieutenant Commander Van Gelder.

"It's not me he wants," Van Gelder said. "It's my trusty stillson wrench. As if he doesn't have a dozen aboard."

"I wouldn't miss this," Hawkins said. He looked at Benson and Wickram. "I'm sure you gentlemen wouldn't want to miss this either. It will, after all, be a historic moment when, for the first time in history, they drop a live atomic mine on the deck of a ship."

"You have a problem, Captain Montgomery?" the admiral asked. Montgomery, winch stopped, was leaning over the guardrail and looking down at the fuselage, which had been raised to its previous position with its cargo deck just above the level of the sea. "You look a mite despondent."

"I am not looking despondent, Admiral. I am looking thoughtful. The next step is to hoist the bomb from the plane. After that, we have to load it aboard the *Angelina*. And then the *Angelina* sails away. Correct?" Hawkins nodded and Montgomery wet his forefinger and held it up. "To sail away you require wind. Unfortunately and most inconveniently the Meltemi has died completely."

"It has, hasn't it?" Hawkins said. "Most inconsiderate, I must say. Well, if we manage to get the bomb aboard the *Angelina* without blowing ourselves to smithereens we'll just tow it away."

"How will we do that, sir?" Van Gelder said.

"The *Ariadne*'s whaler. Not the engine, of course. We row."

"How do we know that the cunning little brain of this explosive device can differentiate between the repeated creaking of oars and the pulse of an engine? After all, sir, it is primarily an acoustic device."

"Then we'll go back to the naval days of yore. Muffled oars."

"But the *Angelina* displaces between eighty and a hundred tons, sir. Even with the best will and the strongest backs in the world it wouldn't be possible to make as much as one nautical mile in an hour. And that's with men continuously pulling with all their strength. Even the strongest, fittest and most highly trained racing crews

—Oxford, Cambridge, Thames Tideway—approach complete exhaustion after twenty minutes. Not being Oxbridge blues, our limit would probably be nearer ten minutes. Half a nautical mile, if we're lucky. And then, of course, the periods between successive onsets of exhaustion would become progressively shorter. Cumulative effects, if you follow me, sir. A quarter of a mile an hour. It's close on a hundred miles to the Kasos Strait."

"When it comes to comfort and encouragement," Hawkins said, "I couldn't ask for a better man to have around. Bubbling over with optimism. Professor Wotherspoon, you live and sail in these parts. What's your opinion."

"It's been an unusual night, but this is a perfectly normal morning. Zero wind. The Etesian wind—the Meltemi as they call it in these parts—starts up around about noon. Comes from the north or northwest."

"What if the wind comes from the south or southeast instead?" Van Gelder said. "It would be impossible for the rowers to make any headway against it. The reverse, rather. Can't you just picture it, the *Angelina* being driven onto the rocks of Santorini?"

"Job's comforter," Hawkins said. "Would it be too much to ask you kindly to cease and desist?"

"Not Job, sir, nor his comforter. I see myself more in the role of Cassandra."

"Why Cassandra?"

"Beautiful daughter of Priam, king of Troy,"

Denholm said. "The prophecies of the princess, though always correct, were decreed by Apollo never to be believed."

"I'm not much of one for Greek mythology," Montgomery said. "Had it been a leprechaun or a brownie, now, I might have listened. As it is, we have work to do. Mr. Danforth"—this to his chief officer—"detail half a dozen men, a dozen, to haul the *Angelina* round to our port quarter. Once the bomb has been removed we can pull the fuselage forward and the *Angelina* can then move forward in her turn to take its place."

Under Montgomery's instructions, the derrick hook was detached from the lifting ring and the derrick itself angled slightly aft until the hook dangled squarely over the center of the rectangular opening that had been cut in the fuselage. Montgomery, Van Gelder and Carrington descended the companionway to the top of the fuselage, Van Gelder with his stillson, Carrington with two adjustable rope grommets to which were attached two slender lengths of line, one eight feet in length, the other perhaps four times as long. Van Gelder and Carrington lowered themselves into the cargo bay and slipped and secured the grommets over the tapered ends of the mine while Montgomery remained above, guiding the winch driver until the lifting fork was located precisely over the center of the mine. The hook was lowered until it was four feet above the mine.

None of the eight securing clamp nuts offered more than a token resistance to Van Gelder's stillson and as each clamp came free Carrington tightened or loosened the pressure on the two shorter ropes which had been attached to the hook. Within three minutes the atomic mine was free of all restraints that had attached it to the bulkhead and floor of the cargo bay and in less than half that time it had been winched upward, slowly and with painstaking care, until it was clear of the plane's fuselage. The two longer ropes attached to the grommets were thrown up onto the deck of the *Kilcharran*, where they were firmly held to ensure that the mine was kept in a position precisely parallel to the hull of the ship.

Montgomery climbed aboard and took over the winch. The mine was hoisted until it was almost level with the ship's deck and then, by elevating the angle of the derrick, carefully brought alongside until it was resting against the rubber-cushioned sides of the *Kilcharran*, a maneuver that was necessary to ensure that the mine did not snag against the port stays of the foremast of the *Angelina* when that vessel was brought alongside.

It took what seemed line an unconscionably long time—in fact, it took just over half an hour —to bring the *Angelina* alongside. Hauling the plane's fuselage forward to leave space for the lugger had been a quick and simple task, but then, because of the supporting air bags, the fuselage was in a state of neutral buoyancy and one man could have accomplished the task with ease. But the *Angelina* displaced upward of eighty tons and even the dozen men assigned to the task of towing it found it a laborious task just to get it under way. This difficulty amply confirmed Van Gelder's assertion that towing it any distance at all by a whaler propelled only by oars was a virtual impossibility. Eventually it was brought alongside, the mine gently lowered into its prepared cradle and clamped into position.

"Routine," Montgomery said to Hawkins. If he was experiencing any feelings of relief and satisfaction, and he would have been less than human not to have done, he showed no signs of them. "Nothing should have gone wrong and nothing did go wrong. All we need now is a tiny puff of wind, the lugger's on her way and all our troubles are over."

"Maybe all our troubles are just beginning," Van Gelder said.

Hawkins looked at him suspiciously. "And what, may we ask, are we expected to gather from that cryptic remark?"

"There is a tiny puff of wind, sir." Van Gelder wetted a forefinger and held it up. "Unfortunately, it's not from the northwest, it's from the southeast. The beginning, I'm afraid, of what is called the Euros." Van Gelder had assumed a conversational tone. "Reading about it last night. Rare in the summer months but not unknown. I'm sure Professor Wotherspoon will confirm this." Wotherspoon's unsmiling nod did indeed confirm it. "Can turn very nasty, very stormy. Gusting up to Force 7 or 8. I can only assume that the radio operators on the *Kilcharran* and the *Ariadne* have, what shall I say, relaxed their vigilance a bit. Understandable, after what they've been through. Must have been something about it in the weather forecasts. And if this wind increases, and according to the book there is no doubt it will, any attempt to sail or row the *Angelina* anywhere will end up with her banging not against the rocks of Santorini, as I suggested, but against those of Sikinos or Folegandros, which I believe are rather sparsely populated. But if the Euros backs more to the east, which I understand it occasionally does, then it would bang into Milos. Five thousand people inhabit Milos."

"I speak with restraint, Van Gelder," Hawkins said. "I don't exactly see myself in the role of an ancient Roman emperor but you do know what happened to messengers that brought bad news to them?"

"They got their heads chopped off."

Bearers of bad news were having a hard time of it on both sides of the Atlantic that morning.

The President of the United States was no longer a young man and at half past five on that morning in the Oval Office he was showing every year of his age. The lines of care and concern were deeply entrenched in his face and the skin, beneath the permanent tan, had a grayish tinge to it. But he was alert enough and his eyes were as clear as could be expected of an elderly man who had had no sleep whatsoever that night.

"I am beginning, gentlemen, to feel almost as

sorry for myself and ourselves as I am for those unfortunates in Santorini." The "gentlemen" he was addressing were the Chairman of the Joint Chiefs of Staff, Richard Hollison of the FBI, John Heiman, the Defense Secretary, and Sir John Travers, the British ambassador. "I suppose I should apologize for bringing you all together at this hour of the morning, but, frankly, I have no decency left in me. I'm right at the undisputed top of my self-pity list." He shuffled through some papers on his desk. "Admiral Hawkins and his men are sitting on top of a ticking time bomb and it seems that nature and circumstances are conspiring to thwart their every attempt to rid themselves of this canker in their midst. With his latest report I had thought that I had reached the ultimate nadir. Inevitably, I was wrong." He looked sorrowfully at the deputy director of the FBI. "You had no right to do this to me, Richard."

"I am sorry about that, Mr. President." Hollison may well have meant what he said but the sorrow was completely masked by the expression and tone of bitter anger. "It's not just bad news, it's shattering news. Shattering for you, shattering for me, most of all shattering for the general. I still can hardly bring myself to believe it."

"I might be prepared to believe it," Sir John Travers said, "and might well be prepared to be shattered along with the best of you. If, that is, I had the slightest idea what you are talking about."

"And *I* am sorry about that," the President said.

"We have not really been remiss, there just hasn't been time yet. Richard, the ambassador has not yet read the relevant documents. Could you put him in the picture, please."

"That shouldn't take too long. It's a damn ugly picture, Sir John, because it reflects badly—just how badly it's only now beginning to dawn on me—on both Americans in general and the Pentagon in particular.

"The central figure in the scenario, of whom you have of course heard, is a certain Adamantios Spyros Andropulous, who is rapidly emerging as an international criminal of staggering proportions. As you know, he is at present being held aboard the frigate *Ariadne*. He is an exceptionally wealthy man—I'm talking merely of hundreds of millions of dollars; it could be billions for all I know—and he has money, laundered money under false names, hidden away in various deposit accounts all over the world. Marcos of the Philippines and Duvalier of Haiti are, or were, rather good at this sort of thing, but they're being found out; they should have employed a real expert like Andropulous."

"He can't be all that expert, Richard," Sir John said. "You've found out about him."

"A chance in a million. In any but the most exceptional circumstances he would have taken the secret to the grave with him. And I didn't find out about him—there is no possible way I ever could have—and no credit whatsoever goes to us. That he was found out is due entirely to two things—an extraordinary stroke of luck and an extraordinary degree of astuteness by those aboard the *Ariadne*. I have, incidentally, have had cause to revise my earlier—and I must admit prejudiced and biased—opinion of Admiral Hawkins. He insists that none of the credit belongs to him but to the captain and two of his officers aboard the *Ariadne*. It takes quite a man to insist on that sort of thing.

"Among his apparently countless worldwide deposits Andropulous had tucked away eighteen million dollars in a Washington bank through an intermediary or nominee by the name of George Skepertzis. This nominee had transferred over a million dollars apiece to the accounts of two men registered in the bank as Thomas Thompson and Kyriakos Katzanevakis. The names, inevitably, are fictitious—no such people exist. The only bank clerk who could identify all three men, inasmuch as he was the person who had handled all three accounts, had left the bank. We tracked him down—he was understandably a bit upset about being dragged out of his bed at midnight—and showed him a group of photographs. Two of them he recognized immediately but none of the photographs remotely resembled the man going by the name of George Skepertzis.

"But he was able to give us some additional—and very valuable—information about Skepertzis, who seemed to have taken him into some limited degree of confidence. No reason why he shouldn't of course. Skepertzis has—had—every reason to believe that his tracks were completely covered. This was approximately two months ago. He wanted to know about the banking facilities in certain specified towns in the United States and Mexico. The bank clerk—his name is Bradshaw —gave him what information he could. It took Bradshaw about a week to find out the details Skepertzis wanted. I should imagine that he was well rewarded for his labors, although, of course, Bradshaw didn't say so. There were no criminal charges that we could have laid against him for that—not that we would, even if we could have.

"Bradshaw provided our agent with the names and addresses of the banks concerned. We checked those against two lists regarding Andropulous's banking activities that we had just received from the *Ariadne* and Greek Intelligence—a third, if you count Interpol. Skepertzis had made inquiries about banks in five cities and, lo and behold and to nobody's surprise, all five also appeared on the lists concerning Andropulous.

"We instituted immediate inquiries. Bankers— especially senior banking officials—have profound objections to being woken in the middle of the night but among our eight thousand FBI agents in the United States we have some very tough and persistent individuals who are also very good at putting the fear of God into even the most law-abiding citizens. And we have some very good friends in Mexico. It turns out that our friend Skepertzis has bank accounts in all five cities. All under his own name."

"You're ahead of me here," the President said. "This is news to me. When did you find this out?"

"Just over half an hour ago. I'm sorry, Mr. President, but there just hasn't been the time to confirm everything and tell you until now. In two of those banks—in Mexico City and San Diego—we struck gold. In each of those banks close to three-quarters of a million dollars has been transferred to the accounts of a certain Thomas Thompson and a certain Kyriakos Katzanevakis. It's a measure of those two gentlemen's belief in their immunity to investigation that they hadn't even bothered to have changed their names. Not that that would have mattered in the long run—not after we had got around to circulating photographs. One final point of interest. Two weeks ago the bank in Mexico City received a draft of two million dollars in favor of George Skepertzis from a reputable, or supposedly reputable, bank in Damascus, Syria. A week later exactly the same amount was transferred to a certain Philip Trypanis in Greece. We have the name of the Athens bank and have asked Greek Intelligence to find out who or what Trypanis is or for whom he is fronting. A sure bet that he is a pal of Andropulous."

A silence ensued, a silence that was long and profound and more than a little gloomy. It was the President himself who finally broke it.

"A provocative tale, is it not, Sir John?"

"Provocative, indeed. Richard had the right term for it—shattering."

"But—well, don't you have any questions?"

"No."

The President looked at him in near-disbelief. "Not a single question?"

"Not even one, Mr. President."

"But surely you must want to know the identities of Thompson and Katzanevakis?"

"I don't want to know. If we must refer to them at all I'd rather just refer to them as the general and the admiral." He looked at Hollison. "That would be about right, Richard?"

"I'm afraid so. A general and an admiral. Your Admiral Hawkins, Sir John, is smarter than your average bear."

"I would agree. But you have to be fair to yourselves. He had access to information that you hadn't had until now. I, too, have an advantage that you people lack. You're deep in the middle of the wood. I'm on the outside looking in.

"Two things, gentlemen. As a representative of Her Majesty's government I am bound to report any developments of significance to the Foreign Office and the Cabinet. But if I specifically lack certain information, such as specific names, then I can't very well report them, can I? We ambassadors have the power to exercise a very wide range of discretion. In this particular instance, I choose to exercise that discretion.

"The second point is that you all seem convinced—there appears to be a certain doom-laden certainty about this—that this affair, this top-level treason, if you will, is bound to become public knowledge. I have one simple question. Why?"

"Why? Why?" The President shook his head as if bemused or stunned by the naïveté of the question. "Goddamnit, Sir John, it's bound to come out. It's inevitable. How else are we going to explain things away? If we are at fault, if we are the guilty party, we must in all honesty openly confess to that guilt. We must stand up and be counted."

"We have been friends for some years now, Mr. President. Friends are allowed to speak openly?"

"Of course, of course."

"Your sentiments, Mr. President, do you the greatest possible credit but hardly reflect what, fortunately or unfortunately, goes on in the more rarefied strata of international diplomacy. I am not speaking of deception and deviousness, I *am* referring to what is practical and politic. It's bound to come out, you say. Certainly it will—but only if the President of the United States decides that it must. How, you ask, are we going to explain things away? Simple. We don't. You give me one valid reason why we should move this matter into the realm of public domain or, as you appear to suggest, make a clean breast of things, and I'll give you half a dozen reasons—reasons equally valid if not more so—why we shouldn't." Sir John paused as if to marshal his facts but was, in fact, merely waiting for one of the four intent listeners to voice an objection; he had already marshaled his facts.

"I think, Mr. President, that it might do us no harm to hear what Sir John has to say." Hollison smiled. "Who knows, we might even learn something. As the senior ambassador of a vastly experienced Foreign Office, it seems likely that Sir John must have gained some little expertise along the way."

"Thank you, Richard. Bluntly and undiplomatically, Mr. President, you have a duty not to speak out. There is nothing whatsoever to be gained, and a very great deal to be lost. At best, you will be hanging out a great deal of dirty washing in public and all to no avail, to no purpose; at worst, you will be providing invaluable ammunition for your enemies. Such open and, if I may say so, ill-advised confession will achieve at best an absolute zero and at worst a big black minus for you, the Pentagon and the citizens of America. The Pentagon, I am sure, is composed of honorable men. Sure, it may have its quota of the misguided, the incompetent, even the downright stupid; name me any large and powerful bureaucratic elite that has never had such a quota. All that matters, finally and basically, is that they *are* honorable men and I see no earthly justification for dragging the reputations of honorable men through the dust because we have discovered two rotten apples at the bottom of the barrel.

"You yourself, Mr. President, are in an even

worse position. You have devoted a considerable deal of your presidential time to combating terrorism in every shape and form. How will it look to the world if it comes out that two senior members of your armed forces have been actively engaged in promoting terrorism for material gain? You may hardly know the two gentlemen concerned but they will, of course, be elevated to the status of highly trusted aides, and that's just looking on the bright side. On the dark side, you will be accused not only of harboring men who are engaged in terrorism but of aiding, abetting and inciting them to new levels of terrorism. Can't you just see the headlines smeared across the front pages of the tabloids and yellow press throughout the world? By the time they have finished with you, you will be remembered in history for one thing and one thing only, the ultimate byword for hypocrisy, the allegedly noble and high-principled President who had spent his life in encouraging and promoting the one evil he had sworn to destroy. Throughout the countries of the world that dislike or fear America because of its power, authority and wealth—and that, like it or not, means most countries—your reputation would lie in tatters. Because of your exceptionally high level of popularity in your own country you will survive but I hardly think that that consideration would affect you. What would and should affect you is that your campaign against terrorism would be irrevocably destroyed. No phoenix would arise from those particular ashes. As a world force for justice and decency you would be a spent man. To put it in the most undiplomatic terms, sir, to go ahead as you propose to do you'd have to be more than slightly off your rocker."

The President stared into the middle distance for quite some time, then said in a voice that was almost plaintive, "Does anyone else here think I'm off my rocker?"

"Nobody thinks you're off your rocker, Mr. President," the general said. "Least of all, I would say, Sir John here. He is merely saying what our unfortunately absent Secretary of State would advocate if he were here. Both gentlemen are high on pragmatism and cold logic and low on unconsidered and precipitate action. Maybe I'm not the ideal person to be passing judgment on this issue, I would obviously be delighted if whatever reputation the Pentagon has survives intact, but I do feel most strongly that, before jumping off the top of the Empire State Building or whatever, one should give some thought to the fatal and irrevocable consequences."

"I can only nod emphatic agreement," John Heiman, the Defense Secretary, said. "If I may mix two metaphors—if I am mixing them—we have only two options. We can let sleeping dogs lie or let loose the hounds of war. Sleeping dogs never harmed anyone but the hounds of war are an unpredictable bunch. Instead of biting the enemy they may well turn, in this case almost certainly would turn, and savage us."

The President looked at Hollison. "Richard?"

"You're in the card game of your life, Mr. President. You've got only one trump and it's marked 'Silence.'"

"So it's four to one, is it?"

"No, Mr. President," Heiman said, "it's not and you know it. It's five to zero."

"I suppose, I suppose." The President ran a weary hand across his face. "And how do we propose to mount this massive display of silence, Sir John?"

"Sorry, Mr. President. If I am asked for my opinions, I am not, as you have seen, slow to give them. But I know the rules and one of them is that I cannot be a party to formulating the policy of a sovereign state. Decisions are for you and for what is, in effect, your war cabinet here."

A messenger entered and handed a slip of paper to the President. "Dispatch from the *Ariadne*, Mr. President."

"I don't have to brace myself for this," the President said. "As far as dispatches from the *Ariadne* are concerned, I am permanently braced. Someday I'll get some good news from that ship." He read the message. "But not, of course, this time. 'Atomic mine removed from cargo bay of bomber and safely transferred to sailing vessel *Angelina*.' Excellent news as far as it goes but then: 'Unexpected one-eighty-degree change in wind course makes sailing departure impossible. Anticipated delay three to six hours. Hydrogen weapons from plane's cargo bay being transferred to diving ship *Kilcharran*. Expect to complete transfer by nightfall.' End of message. Well, where does that leave us?"

Sir John Travis said, "It leaves you, Mr. President, with a few hours' breathing space."

"Meaning?"

"Masterly inactivity. Nothing that can be profitably done at the moment. I am merely thinking out loud." He looked at the Chairman of the Joint Chiefs of Staff. "Tell me, General, do those two gentlemen in the Pentagon know they are under suspicion. Correction. Do they know that you have proof of their treason?"

"No. And I agree with what you are about to say: No point will be served by acquainting them of that fact at the present moment."

"None. With the President's permission, I would like to retire and ponder the problems of state and international diplomacy. With the aid of a pillow."

The President smiled one of his increasingly rare smiles.

"What a splendid suggestion. I also shall do exactly that. It's close to six now, gentlemen. May I suggest that we gather again at ten-thirty A.M.?"

At two-thirty that afternoon Van Gelder, message sheet in hand, joined Talbot on the bridge of the *Ariadne*.

"Radio from Heraklion, sir. Seems that a Phantom of the Greek Air Force located the diving ship *Taormina* less than ten minutes after taking off from base. It was just east of Avgo Island, which the chart tells me is about forty miles northeast of

Heraklion. Very conveniently positioned to break through the Kasos Strait."

"What direction was it headed?"

"No direction. Having no wish to raise any suspicion, the Greek pilot didn't hang around but he reports that the *Taormina* was stopped in the water."

"Lurking. Lurking, one wonders, for what? Speaking of lurking, what's Jimmy doing at the moment?"

"Last seen, he was lurking with two young ladies in the wardroom. The three A's have retired, to their cabins, presumably for the afternoon. The girls report a far from subtle change in their behavior. They have stopped discussing the predicament they find themselves in, in fact they have stopped discussing anything. They appear unusually calm, relaxed and not very concerned about anything, which may mean that they have philosophically resigned themselves to whatever fate may hold in store or they may have made up their minds about some plan of action, although what that could be I couldn't even begin to imagine."

"What would your guess be, Vincent?"

"A plan of action? I know it's only the slenderest of clues but it's just possible that they may be resting up this afternoon because they don't expect to be doing much resting during the coming night."

"I have the oddest feeling that we won't be doing much resting ourselves tonight."

"Aha! The second sight, sir? Your nonexistent Scottish blood clamoring for recognition."

"When it clamors a bit more, I'll let you know. I just keep wondering about Jenkins's disappearance." A phone rang and Talbot picked it up. "A message for the admiral from the Pentagon? Bring it here." Talbot hung up and gazed out through the for'ard screens of the bridge. The *Angelina*, to protect it from the buffeting of the four-foot-high waves generated by the now very brisk Euros wind from the southeast, had been moved to a position where it lay snugly in the still waters between the bow of the *Ariadne* and the stern of the *Kilcharran*.

"Speaking of the Pentagon, it's only an hour since we told them that we expected the unloading of the hydrogen missiles to be completed by nightfall. And what do we have? A Force 6 and the plane's fuselage streamed out a cable length to the northwest. Lord only knows when the unloading will be finished now. Do you think we should so inform them?"

"I should think not, sir. The President of the United States is a much older man than we are and the kind of cheery communications he has been receiving from the *Ariadne* of late can't be doing his heart any good."

"I suppose you're right. Thank you, Myers."

"Bloody funny signal if you ask me, sir. Can't make head nor tail of it."

"Those things are sent to try us." Talbot waited till Myers had left, then read out the signal.

"'Identity of cuckoos in the nest established. Irrefutable proof that they are linked to your generous benefactor friend. Sincerest congratulations to Admiral Hawkins and the officers of the *Ariadne*.'"

"Recognition at last," Van Gelder said.

"You are the last to arrive, Sir John," the President said. "I have to advise you that we have already made up our minds what to do."

"A very difficult decision, I assume, Mr. President. Probably the most difficult you have ever been called upon to make."

"It has been. Now that the decision is made and is irrevocable, you can no longer be accused of meddling with the affairs of a sovereign state. What would you have done, Sir John?"

"Perfectly straightforward. Exactly what you have done. No one is to be informed except two people and those two people are to be informed that the President has suspended them indefinitely from duty, pending the investigation of allegations and statements that have been laid against them."

"Well, I'll be damned." The President spoke without heat. "Instead of sleeping all the time I spent a couple of hours wrestling with my conscience to arrive at the same conclusion."

"It was inevitable, sir. You had no option. And I would point out that it's easy enough for us to arrive at decisions. You, and only you, can give the executive order."

"I will not insult your intelligence by asking if you are aware what this executive order means."

"I am perfectly aware of what it means. Now that my opinion is no longer called for, I have no hesitation in saying that I would have done exactly the same thing. It is a death sentence and it can be no consolation at all that you will not be called upon to carry out, or to order to be carried out, the execution of that death sentence."

9

"Manhattan Project?" Admiral Hawkins said. "What on earth does she mean by Manhattan Project?"

"I don't know, sir," Denholm said. "Eugenia doesn't know either. She just caught the words as she walked into the wardroom. Only Andropulous, Alexander and Aristotle were there. The phrase was repeated twice and she thought it odd enough—I think it's very odd, too—to pass it on to me. When they became aware of her presence the subject was switched. She said that whatever the nature of the subject was they seemed to find it rather amusing."

Talbot said, "Even Alexander was amused?"

"Humor, sir, is not Alexander's forte. Nobody's seen him smile since he came aboard the *Ar-*

iadne; I would doubt if anyone has ever seen him smile. Besides, it was Alexander who was discussing the subject. Maybe he doesn't laugh at his own jokes."

"I know you know something about those things, Denholm," Hawkins said. "Doesn't it suggest anything to you?"

"Zero, sir. The immediate and obvious—far too obvious—connection is the atom bomb. The Manhattan Project, of course, was that immensely long, immensely complicated and immensely expensive project that led to the invention of the atom bomb. 'Manhattan' was only a code word. The actual research was carried out in New Mexico and Nevada or thereabouts. I'm sorry, sir, but the significance, the relevance of the phrase in our present situation, quite escapes me."

"At least I've got company," Hawkins said. He picked up two slips of paper from his table in the admiral's cabin. "Those two messages have come in since we saw you last. In this case, I don't think their significance will escape you."

"Ah! This one from the White House itself. 'Two of your philantropist's beneficiaries are no longer with us. Beneficiary A has been involved in a fatal automobile accident.'" Denholm looked up from the paper. "Has he, now? For beneficiary A, I take it we can read either Admiral X or General Y. Did he fall, did he jump or was he pushed?" He looked at the paper again. "And I see that Beneficiary B has just disappeared. Again

I assume that Beneficiary B was either X or Y. How very inconvenient for them, how very convenient for us." Denholm looked from Hawkins to Talbot. "From the very restrained wording I take it that this news is not to be broadcast from the housetops."

"I shouldn't have thought so," Hawkins said. "We have already arranged for the coded original to be destroyed."

I take it, then, sir, that speculation about their abrupt departure is pointless."

"Not only pointless but needless. They have fallen upon their swords. One does not wish to sound cynical or stand in condemnation but it's probably the only faintly honorable thing they have done for a long time. The second signal, Denholm?"

"The one from Heraklion. Interesting, sir. It seems that the *Taormina's* last port of call was Tobruk. Furthermore, although it's registered in Panama, it appears to be permanently based in Tobruk. It's more than interesting, it's intriguing, especially considering that that well-know philanthropist sitting in our wardroom seems to have considerable business interests in Tripoli. It's most damnable frustrating, sir."

"What is?"

"That we haven't a single shred of evidence to adduce against him, far less proof."

"I have this feeling," Talbot said, "that neither evidence nor proof will ever be required. Andropulous will never come to trial."

Hawkins looked at him for a few thoughtful moments. "That's the second time you've said that, Captain. You have access to some information that we lack?"

"Not at all, sir. Maybe I've just got blind faith in this blindfolded goddess of justice. You know, the lady who holds the scales in her hands." Talbot smiled. "Or maybe, as Van Gelder keeps on hinting, I have some traces of Highland blood in me. Says I'm fey, the second sight or some nonsense like that. Ah, the man himself."

"A radio message from Greek Intelligence," Van Gelder said. He proffered the paper he held in hand.

"Just tell me," Hawkins said. "Gently. I'm becoming allergic to bad news."

"Not all that bad, sir. Not for us, at any rate. Says that someone attached to the Department for Middle East and North African Affairs—they carefully don't give his name, I suppose he's a minister of some sort, I suppose we could find out easily enough but is seems unimportant—took off by government plane on a routine visit to Canea, the town close by the Suda Bay air base. Never got there. But at exactly the time he should have got there a patrolling Greek Mirage spotted a plane very like the one he was flying in—too much of a coincidence for it not to have been the same plane—passing directly over Heraklion."

"So, of course," Talbot said, "you consulted the chart and arrived at the conclusion that he was heading for some place. What place?"

"Tobruk."

"And you also arrived at the conclusion that he wouldn't be coming back from there?"

"Allowing for the vagaries of human nature, sir, I would not have thought so. Greek Intelligence have also established the fact that the vanishing minister, if minister he was, held an account at the same Athens bank that Philip Trypanis honors with his business. It would appear, to coin a phrase, that they are now hot on the trail of Mr. Trypanis. Whether they nab Mr. Trypanis or not hardly seems a matter of concern for us."

"I would think," Hawkins said. "if our philanthropist friend in the wardroom knew of the fate of his pal in government here and those of A and B—or X and Y—in Washington his humor might be in marked abeyance by now. And if he knew that we knew of the *Taormina* and that it's home base was Tobruk, he would be downright thoughtful. Was that all, Van Gelder?"

"On the subject, sir, yes. Captain Montgomery, Professor Wotherspoon and I have been discussing the weather."

"You have?" Hawkins looked at him with suspicion. "Don't tell me that Cassandra has you in her clutches again?"

"Certainly not, sir. The Euros has died away. Completely. We suspect it will be only a matter of time before the weather returns to normal. A very short time. Latest reports confirm that. The *Angelina*, at the present moment, is lying between our ship and the *Kilcharran*, facing northwest, of course—we won't be able to sail her out of her present position. It might be wise to tow her alongside us now."

"Of course," Talbot said. "See to it now, would you, Number One. After that, let us gather for the last supper."

Van Gelder looked through the opened doorway. "It's already getting dark, sir. You don't feel like waiting for the dawn before we take off?"

"Nothing I'd like better than to wait for the dawn. But the sooner we take off, the easier the heads along the Potomac will sleep. Not to mention, of course, those on the *Kilcharran* and *Ariadne*."

Denholm looked from Talbot to Van Gelder. His face registered an expression of near-incredulity.

"Am I to understand, Captain, that you and Lieutenant Commander Van Gelder are sailing on the *Angelina*?"

Talbot shook his head. "I suppose it had to come to this, Number One. Junior officers questioning our nautical expertise."

"I don't understand, sir. Why on earth are you and Number One going along on the *Angelina*? I mean—"

"We are not going along on the *Angelina*. We are taking the *Angelina*. Professor Wotherspoon and his wife are the people who are not going. They don't know that yet, of course. The good professor is going to be very unhappy but it's difficult to please everybody."

"I see, sir. Yes, I see. I should have guessed. I'd like to come along, sir."

"Yes and no. You shall come along, but not on the *Angelina*. You will take the launch. You won't start up the engine until we're at least three miles clear. We don't want, you understand, to precipitate any premature big bangs."

"And then we follow you at that distance?"

"Not so much follow us as circle us—at, of course, the same prudent distance of three miles. Your purpose, again, of course, is to warn off any unsuspecting vessels that come too close."

"And then help tow you back here?"

"When we've dumped the mine and sailed on a sufficiently safe distance, we'll start the engine and head back. A tow would help. Or perhaps the admiral will fetch us in the *Ariadne*. We haven't decided yet and at the moment it's not important. But what I'm about to say *is* important.

"You will take along with you Chief Petty Officer McKenzie, Marine Sergeant Brown and Petty Officer Myers to operate the radio. Most importantly, you will also take with you, suitably wrapped in plastic, the krytron detonation device and conceal it well. I suggest under the floorboards of the wheelhouse. You will instruct Petty Officer Myers to take along the smallest portable transceiver he can lay hands on and conceal it in the same place. Make sure the floorboards are securely nailed down afterward."

"May I ask the reason for this excessive secrecy, sir?"

"You may not, for the excellent reason that I have no reason to give you. The best I can do is to wave a vague hand and say that I am preparing for unforeseen eventualities. The trouble with the unforeseen is that it is unforeseeable. You understand?"

"I think so, sir."

"I suggest you go now and alert your crew. And for God's sake don't let anyone see you wandering around with the krytron under your arm."

Lieutenant Denholm left. Hawkins said, "There are times, Captain, when I feel I have to say, with regret of course, that the truth is not always with you. I mean the truth, the whole truth and nothing but the truth."

"I agree, sir," Van Gelder said. "Sets a very bad example for junior officers."

Talbot smiled. "Be ye as pure as snow ye shall not escape calumny. Something like that. We captains become inured to such injustices. I have the odd feeling—all right, all right, Vincent, let's settle for just a few microscopic traces of Highland blood—that Andropulous is going to be asking the odd casual question at table tonight. I suggest we have Dr. Wickram up here."

Andropulous did indeed have the odd casual question to ask at table that night but he was in no hurry to introduce it. It was not until after they had finished the main course that he said, "We do not wish to pry, Captain, or ask questions about purely naval matters which should be none of our concern. But whatever *is* happening surely does concern us, whether directly or indirectly, and we are but human and very, very curious. We can all see that the *Angelina* is alongside with that highly suspect atomic mine lashed down in its cradle on the deck. I thought the intention was to sail it away with all possible speed."

"We shall be doing just that, Mr. Andropulous. In the fullness of time, by which I mean after we've finished dinner. You will not be happy until it is gone?"

"I confess I will feel a considerable degree of relief when I see the *Angelina* disappearing over the horizon, and with a clear sky and an almost full moon we should be able to see just that. Selfish? Cowardly? Maybe, maybe not." Andropulous sighed. "I do not see myself in the role of hero."

"I don't see myself as such. No sensible person does."

"But, surely—well, that atomic mine is still highly unstable, is it not?"

"I don't think it's quite so highly dangerous as it was. But why ask me? You're sitting next to the expert."

"Of course. Dr. Wickram. How do you see things now, sir?"

"The captain is right, or I hope he is. The radioactive emanations of the hydrogen missiles, from which of course the atomic mine is now separated, have an extremely limited range. They are no longer affecting the mine, which should now be slowly beginning to stabilize itself. But I have to emphasize that it's a slow process."

"How long will it be before it has fully stabilized itself? By which I mean when will it reach a condition when a passing vessel's engines will have no effect on it?"

"Ah. Well, now." Wickram's tone was the verbal equivalent of a shrug. "As I've said, we're in the realms of the unknown, the untested, but I have been making some calculations. Difficult calculations involving some rather advanced mathematics, so I won't bother you with those, but my estimate is that the mine should be quite safe in twelve hours at the most. Possible even in six hours. At a lesser time than that, well, the risk would be unacceptably high."

"Damn you to hell, Talbot," Wotherspoon said. His voice was low and controlled but the ivory-knuckled fists showed the depth of his anger. "It's *my* boat you're talking about. It's not the property of your damned Navy!"

"I am aware of that, Professor, and I'm most damnably sorry about it." Talbot was with Hawkins, Wotherspoon and his wife in the admiral's cabin. "But you are not coming along. Did you honestly imagine that the Royal Navy would idly stand by and let you, civilians, risk your lives for us?" Talbot smiled. "It's not only our duty but we're getting paid for it."

"It's not only bloody high-handed, it's piracy! Hijack. The sort of illegal behavior you're sworn to destroy. You are, of course, prepared to resort to force in order to restrain me."

"If we have to, yes." Talbot nodded to the open darkened doorway. Wotherspoon turned, caught sight of three large figures half hidden in the gloom. When he turned back, he was literally speechless with fury. "It's the last thing we want to do." Talbot said, "and it's totally unnecessary." He let an element of coldness creep into his voice. "Quite frankly, Wotherspoon, my primary concern is not your welfare. I think you're being most extraordinarily selfish and totally inconsiderate. How long have you been married, Mrs. Wotherspoon?"

"How long have—" She tried to smile but her heart wasn't in it. "Almost six months."

"Less than six months." Talbot looked at Wotherspoon without enthusiasm. "And yet you're willing to expose her to danger and and—the chance is very real—to send her to death because your stiff-necked pride has been wounded. You must be proud of yourself. Do you really want to go, Mrs. Wotherspoon?"

"Angelina." The correction was automatic and this time she did smile, almost certainly because of the incongruity of it in the circumstances. "You put me in an impossible situation." She paused, then went on quickly. "No. No, you don't. I *don't* want to go. I don't want James to go either. Delving around in antiquities is our business, not violence and death. Heaven knows, I'm no latter-day Amazon and if there are any dragons waiting around to be killed I don't want my husband to be St. George. *Please* James."

Hawkins spoke for the first time. "I make no appeal to your emotions, Professor. All I ask you is to put yourself in Commander Talbot's position. I think you would agree it is a pretty impossible one."

"Yes." Wotherspoon had unclenched his fists. "I see that."

"I think three signals are in order, John," Hawkins said. The Wotherspoons had left. "One to the White House, one to General Carson in Rome and one to Rear Admiral Blyth. The same signal, coded of course, to each. How about 'Settled weather with favorable northwest wind. *Angelina* about to sail with armed mine. Transfer of hydrogen missiles from plane to *Kilcharran* continuing smoothly.' That should fit the bill?"

"Admirably. It should come as quite a shock to them all."

"We haven't of late, I must admit, been sending them much in the way of good news."

A small knot of interested spectators were gathered around the head of the gangway, the foot of which offered easy access to both the stern of the *Angelina*, whose sails were already hoisted, and the bow of the *Ariadne's* launch. Among the more interested of the spectators was Andropulous.

He turned to Talbot and said, "How much longer now, Captain?"

"Ten minutes. Thereabouts."

Andropulous shook his head as if in disbelief. "And then all our troubles will be over?"

"It's beginning to look that way, isn't it?"

"It is indeed. Tell me, why is the launch there?"

"Simple. It's coming with us."

"Going with you? I don't understand. Won't the sound of its engines—"

"Maybe trigger off the mine? The launch won't start up until we're at least three miles clear. It will then proceed to circle us, again at a distance of three miles, to warn off any vessels—powered vessels, that is—that threaten to come too close to us. We haven't come this far, Mr. Andropulous, to take any chances."

"The thought, the precaution, never occurred to me. Alas, I fear I will never make a man of action."

Talbot gave him what Andropulous misinterpreted as a kindly smile. "One cannot be all things to all men, sir."

"You are ready to go, Captain?" Hawkins said. He had just joined them.

"A few minutes, sir. Sails are filling rather nicely, aren't they?"

"*You* are going, Captain?" Andropulous seemed a trifle disconcerted.

"Certainly. I've always rather fancied myself as the skipper on an Aegean lugger. You seem rather surprised, Mr. Andropulous."

"I am. Rather, I was. But not now." He looked down to the deck of the *Angelina*, where Van

Gelder was adjusting a halyard on the foresail. "And of course, inevitably, Lieutenant Commander Van Gelder. Handpicked men, eh, Captain. Handpicked by yourself, of course. I congratulate you. I also salute you. I suspect that this is a much more dangerous mission than you have led us to understand, a mission so perilous that you have chosen not to delegate some members of your crew to carry it out."

"Nonsense, Mr. Andropulous. You exaggerate. Well, Admiral, we're off. Taking a median estimate on Dr. Wickram's time limits we should be disposing of this mine in nine hours' time—six A.M. tomorrow. If the wind holds—there's no guarantee that it will, of course—we'll be well on our way to the Kasos Strait by then."

Hawkins nodded. "And with luck—although I don't see why the factor luck should enter into it—we should be picking you up in the early afternoon tomorrow. We shall remain with Captain Montgomery until he has finished loading the hydrogen missiles and until the destroyer I've radioed for comes to pick him up and escort him to Thessalonica. That should be between nine and ten in the morning. Then we'll come looking for you." He turned his head. "You're off, Mr. Andropulous? I should have thought you would have remained to witness this rather historic moment."

"I intend to do just that. I also intend to record this historic moment. I go to fetch my trusty Leica. Well, Lieutenant Denholm's trusty Leica. He lent it to me less than an hour ago."

247

Talbot chatted briefly with Hawkins, said his good-bye, climbed down the gangway, had a brief word with Denholm on the launch and then boarded the *Angelina*. Van Gelder had already pulled in and coiled the bow rope. Talbot stooped over the cleat on the poop deck to do the same with the stern rope when he became aware of a certain commotion and exclamations about his head. He straightened and looked up.

Andropulous had made his reappearance, not with his trusty Leica, but with what was probably an equally trusty and much more unpleasant Navy Colt .44, the muzzle of which was pressed against the temple of a plainly terrified Angelina Wotherspoon. Behind him loomed Achmed, Alexander and Aristotle, the men similarly armed and with the muzzles of their pistols similarly pointed at the temples of Irene Charial and her friend Eugenia, neither of whom looked any happier than Angelina.

"Don't cast off quite yet, Captain," Andropulous said. "We're coming with you."

"What in God's name is the meaning of this?" Hawkin's expression reflected an equal degree of shock and anger. "Have you taken leave of your senses?"

"We have not taken leave of our senses. We are just taking leave of you." He jabbed Angelina's temple with a force that made her gasp with pain. "After you, Mrs. Wotherspoon."

The six of them descended the gangway in succession and boarded the *Angelina*. Andropulous transferred the attention of his Colt from Angelina to Talbot and Van Gelder.

"Nothing rash or heroic or gallant, if you please," Andropulous said. "Especially gallant. It could only have the most distressing consequences, both for you and for the three young ladies."

"Is this a joke?" Talbot said.

"Do I detect a certain loss of composure, a crack in the monolithic calm? If I were you, Captain, I would not take me for a joker."

"I don't." Talbot made no attempt to conceal his bitterness. "I took you for a wealthy businessman and a man of honor. I took you at your face value. I suppose we all learn from our mistakes."

"You are too late to learn from this mistake. You are correct in one respect—I freely confess to being a wealthy businessman. A very wealthy one. As to the second charge?" He shrugged his indifference. "Honor is in the eye of the beholder. Let us not waste time. Instruct this young man"—Denholm, standing in the bow of the launch, was less than six feet away—"to follow his orders precisely. The orders, I understand, that you have given him, Captain. That is, not to start his engines until we have put three miles away from him and then to circle us, at that same distance, to fend off unwanted intruders."

"Lieutenant Denholm understands his orders perfectly clearly."

"In which case, cast off."

The wind was fresh, but not strong, and it took

the *Angelina* quite some time to overcome its initial inertia and reach a speed of three or four knots. Slowly the *Ariadne* dropped astern and after fifteen minutes it was at least a mile distant.

"Excellent," Andropulous said. "Rather gratifying, is it not, when things go exactly according to plan." There was no hint of undue satisfaction in his voice. "Tell me, Commander Talbot, would you believe me when I say that I am genuinely fond, very fond, of my niece and her friend Eugenia and might even come to regard Mrs. Wotherspoon in the same light?"

"I don't know why I should believe you and I don't see why it should concern me."

"And would you believe me when I say I wouldn't harm a hair of their heads?"

"I'm afraid I do."

"Afraid?"

"Others wouldn't believe it, or wouldn't know whether to believe it or not. Which makes them perfect hostages."

"Exactly. I don't need to say that they will come to no harm at my hands." He looked thoughtfully at Talbot. "You are singularly incurious as to the reasons for my conduct."

"I am very curious. But one does not become a wealthy businessman by engaging in idle tittle-tattle. If I were to ask you, you would tell me exactly what you wanted to tell me. No more, no less."

"How very true. Now, a different point entirely. The three young ladies pose absolutely no threat to me. You and Van Gelder are a very different kettle of fish. My three friends and I regard you as highly dangerous individuals. We think you are capable of concocting devious and cunning plans and using a great deal of violence in putting those plans to the test, if, that is, you thought there was the slightest chance of success. You will understand, therefore, that we will have to immobilize you. I will remain by the wheel here. You two gentlemen, accompanied by the three ladies, will proceed to the saloon, where Aristotle, who, as you will readily understand, is very good at knots, will tie you hand and foot, while Alexander, who is every bit as proficient with a gun as Aristotle is with ropes, will ensure that prodeedings are conducted in a peaceful fashion."

Hawkins was bent over Professor Wotherspoon, who was lying half propped up on a sofa in the wardroom. Wotherspoon, dazed and making odd choking noises that were partway between moans and curses, was struggling to open his eyes. Finally, with the aid of his fingers, he managed to do just that.

"What the hell has happened?" The watchers had to strain to catch his words, which were no more than an asthmatic croak. "Where am I?"

"Take this." Hawkins put an arm around his shoulders and a glass of brandy to his lips. Wotherspoon sipped, gagged, then drained the contents.

"What *has* happened?"

"You've been banged over the back of the head," Grierson said, "and not lightly either. 'Sapped,' I believe, is the current term. By the butt of the revolver, I should guess."

Wotherspoon struggled to a sitting position. "Who?"

"Andropulous," Hawkins said. "Or one of his criminal friends. Some more brandy is in order, Doctor?"

"Normally, no," Grierson said. "In this case, yes. I know the back of your head must hurt badly, Professor, but don't touch it. Bruised, bleeding, puffy, but no fracture."

"Andropulous has hijacked your vessel," Hawkins said. "Along, of course, with the atomic mine. He has also taken hostages."

Wotherspoon nodded and winced at the pain it caused him. "My wife, of course, is one of them."

"I am sorry. Along with Irene Charial and her friend Eugenia. There was no way we could stop them."

"Did you try?"

"Would you have tried if you saw the barrel of a Colt screwed against your wife's temple? And two other guns screwed against the temples of the two other ladies?"

"I hardly think so." Wotherspoon shook his head. "I'm trying to come to terms with the situation. With a head like an overripe pumpkin about to burst, it's not easy. Talbot and Van Gelder. What's happened to them?"

"We don't know, of course. Handcuffed or some such, I should imagine."

"Or permanently disposed of. What in God's name is behind all this, Admiral? Do you think this fellow Andropulous has gone off his rocker?"

"By his own standards, he's probably under the impression that he's perfectly sane. We have every reason to believe that he is a long-term and highly professional criminal operating on a hitherto unprecedented international scale. Terrorism and drugs would appear to be his forte. There is no time to go into that at the moment. The immediate point is that Lieutenant Denholm is very shortly leaving in the launch to follow them. Do you feel up to accompanying him?"

"Follow them? Board and capture them? I should say."

"As you as much as said yourself, Professor, your mind isn't yet firing on all cylinders. If the launch were to go within a couple of miles of the *Angelina* its engine beat would probably detonate the atomic mine."

"As you say, I'm not at my best. But if you have any spare rifles or pistols there would be no harm in taking them along. Just in case."

"There will be no firearms. If there were to be any exchange of fire you know where the first bullet would lodge, don't you?"

"Yes. You do put things so nicely. Less than an hour ago you were prepared to restrain me at all costs. You seem to have changed your mind, Admiral."

"It's not my mind that has changed. It's the circumstances."

"A rapid change in circumstances," the President said, "does give one a rather more balanced view of life. I wouldn't go so far as to say that I enjoyed that launch, but then, a couple of hours ago I didn't expect or wish to have any today. Although the memory of the treachery will be with us for a long time I have to admit that the discreet if tragic settlement of the Pentagon question removes a major burden of worry. But that was only a local and, let's face it, a basically selfish concern." He waved the paper he held in his hand. "This, of course, is what matters. The *Angelina*, with this damned bomb aboard, is heading steadily southeast and with every second that passes it is putting another yard between itself and all the horrors of Santorini. It is not too much to say, gentlemen, that a holocaust of unimaginable proportions has been averted." He raised his glass. "I give you a toast, Sir John. The Royal Navy."

The President had barely returned his glass to the table when a messenger entered. The President glanced at him briefly, looked away, then looked at him again. All traces of satisfaction drained from his face.

"Bad news, Johnson?"

"I'm afraid so, Mr. President."

"The worst?"

"Not the worst. But bad enough."

The President took the message, read it in silence, then looked up and said, "I'm afraid our celebrations have been rather premature. The *Angelina* has been hijacked."

Nobody repeated the word "hijacked." Nobody said anything. There didn't seem to be anything so say.

"Message reads: '*Angelina* and armed mine hijacked by Andropulous and three criminal associates. Five hostages taken—Commander Talbot, Lieutenant Commander Van Gelder and three ladies, one of whom is Andropulous's niece. Physically impossible for *Angelina* to return to area, so major danger no longer exists. Will keep you posted hourly. Our major and only concern now recovery of hostages.'"

"Dear me, dear me," Sir John said. "This *is* distressing. Both ominous and confusing. Here we have this madman—or genius; who knows how much truth there is in the old maxim that they are the two sides of the same coin—loose in the Levant with an armed atomic mine aboard. Does he know that it's armed? One rather suspects he doesn't. Where have the three ladies suddenly appeared from and what were they doing aboard one of Her Majesty's frigates in the first place? Why, of all improbabilities, should this villian elect to kidnap his own niece? And why, not to mention how, did this same villain kidnap the captain of the frigate and one of his senior officers? And where does he hope to sail his ship, cargo and prisoners, when he must know that every ship and plane in NATO will be searching for him? But it is obvious he does hope to pull it off. His long and spectacularly successful criminal career, undetected until now, proves that he is a devious, cunning and brilliant operator. He has another scheme in mind. Not a man, as we have now learned to our cost and should have known from his record, to be underestimated."

"One can only hope that Commander Talbot proves to be even more resourceful," the President said.

"I have the uncomfortable feeling," Sir John said, "that at the present moment Talbot is in no position to prove anything."

10

On the hour of midnight, eastern Mediterranean time, Commander Talbot was, in fact, in no position to prove anything and, judging from his uncomfortable position on a sofa in the *Angelina*'s saloon, with his ankles lashed together and his hands bound behind his back, it didn't seem that he would be in a position to prove anything for quite some time to come. Van Gelder was restrained equally uncomfortably at the other end of the sofa. Aristotle, with a wholly unnecessary pistol held loosely across his knee, was seated very comfortably indeed in a large armchair facing the sofa. The three ladies were in smaller armchairs toward the after end of the saloon and didn't look at all comfortable. They hadn't exchanged a word for upward of two hours. There didn't seem to be much to talk about and all three, understandably enough, were preoccupied with their own thoughts.

Talbot said, "Tell Andropulous I want to speak to him."

"Do you now?" Aristotle lowered the glass from which he had been sipping. "You are not in a position, Captain, to give orders to anyone."

"Would you kindly present my compliments to the captain and say I would like to talk to him?"

"That is better." Aristotle rose, crossed to the short flight of steps leading up to the wheelhouse and said something in Greek. Andropulous appeared almost at once. He, too, was needlessly armed. There was a relaxed and confident, even cheerful air about him.

"When you were aboard my ship," Talbot said, "we catered to your every desire. Whatever you wanted, you had but to ask. I wish I could say the same for Greek hospitality. Well, your version of it."

"I think I take your point. It can't be easy for you to lie there and watch Aristotle steadily lowering the level in a bottle of retsina. You are thirsty?"

"Yes."

"That's easily remedied."

In very short order, Aristotle had their bonds quickly and skillfully rearranged, with Talbot's left wrist and Van Gelder's right loosely but securely attached to each other. Their free hands now held a glass apiece.

"I am becoming suspicious, Captain," Andro-pulous said. He neither looked nor sounded suspicious. "You seem totally unconcerned as to the immediate past and the immediate future. I find it very curious indeed."

"There's nothing curious about it. It's your behavior that I find extraordinarily curious, although I have to admit that that is based entirely on my complete ignorance of what is going on. I can't even begin to understand why you should jeopardize your career, perhaps even risk a prison sentence, although I have no doubt that with the kind of money you must possess you wouldn't have too much trouble in bending the law in your direction. Most of all, I don't understand how you can possibly hope to get away with it. By six o'clock, possibly seven, tomorrow morning every ship and plane in NATO will be looking for you and you must know that it will take very little time to locate you."

"You have this famous Royal Navy signal—locate, engage and destroy. Locate, yes. Destroy, no." Andropulous was quite undisturbed. "Not with the kind of cargo and very select group of hostages I have on board. As for jeopardizing my career, well, I think the time comes in many people's lives when they should abandon the old ways and strike out in a fresh direction. Don't you, Captain?"

"Not where I'm concerned. And perhaps, where you are concerned it's not a choice but a necessity. But that's just empty speculation. I really don't know and, to be honest, I no longer care. Could I have some more wine?"

"What are you going to do with us?" Irene Charial was trying to keep her voice steady but the undercurrent of strain was there. "What is going to happen to us?"

"Don't be ridiculous, my dear. Nothing is going to happen to you. You heard me say that to Commander Talbot when we came aboard. Unthinkable that you should come to any harm at my hands."

"Where are you taking us?"

"I'm not taking you anywhere. To what will probably be my lifelong regret, I shall be parting company with you. Within a very short time I shall be transferring you aboard the *Ariadne*'s launch and bidding you farewell."

"And the two officers here? Do you shoot them or just tie their hands up again and throw them overboard?"

"I had looked for more intelligence from my niece," Andropulous said. "If it had been my intention to dispose of them, I should have done so immediately we came aboard."

"What's to stop them from coming after you? You know they can call for help."

"Irene, don't be stupid." Van Gelder grimaced.

"I'm afraid I have to agree with both Van Gelder and your uncle," Talbot said. "You are naïve." He cocked his fingers, pistol fashion. "Poof! Exit engine. Poof! Exit radio."

Andropulous smiled. "As you say, a double poof should do it nicely."

Denholm looked out at the light flickering from the north. "What does the *Angelina* say, Myers?"

"'Stop two miles southeast of us and cut engines.' How shall I answer, sir?"

"We don't have any option. 'Wilco.'" He waited until Myers had triggered the reply, then said, "What's the latest news about the *Taormina*?" The *Ariadne* had been monitoring the radio traffic between the *Angelina* and the *Taormina* for almost three hours and had the position of the *Taormina*—and themselves—pinpointed to within a few hundred yards.

"Just ten miles north of Avgo Island and moving, pretty slowly, north."

"Proceeding with caution." The *Ariadne* had picked up Andropulous's warning to the *Taormina* of the danger of their coming together too soon. "How long before they make contact?"

"Three hours, give or take. A bit longer, I should think, if the *Angelina* stops off alongside for a bit."

"Do you think," Wotherspoon said, "that they might have in mind to sink us, Lieutenant?"

"I would be grateful, Professor, if you didn't even think of such things."

Under the watchful eyes of four men with four guns McKenzie and Brown took and secured the ropes of the *Angelina* as it came alongside. First aboard was Andropulous himself, followed by Angelina Wotherspoon, who immediately seemed bent on strangling the professor, then the two girls, Talbot and Van Gelder with their hands still bound behind their backs and finally Achmed, Alexander and Aristotle, the last carrying a bag.

"We will not stay long," Andropulous said. "One or two small things to attend to first, then we shall be on our way."

"May one ask what is in that bag?" Wotherspoon said. "A delayed-action bomb?"

"Mankind has so little trust in one another these days," Andropulous said. He shook the bag gently and a slight tinkling noise resulted. "To while away the time while you await rescue. Commander Talbot's idea, really. After all, it's your liquor, Wotherspoon. This, I take it, is the radio."

"Do me a last favor," Talbot said. "A favor to all of us. Don't blow it apart with a bullet. Just tap it gently with the butt of your revolver. Similarly with the engine. It requires very little effort to destroy the distribution and the plugs." He nodded toward the armed mine lying in its cradle. "I'm not at all sure how our friend here would react to the explosive crack of a pistol shot."

"A well-taken point," Andropulous said. "We just don't know how temperamental that mine is." He reversed his grip on the pistol, levered open the face plate of the radio and swept the butt across the transistors. It took him scarcely more time to attend to the engine. He next turned his attention to the signaling lamp, smashed it thoroughly and turned to Myers. "Is there a spare?"

Myers swore at him, softly, and Andropulous raised his gun. Talbot said, "Don't be a fool, Myers. Give it to him."

Myers, tight-lipped, handed over a small hand signaling lamp. Andropulous broke the face and threw it into the water. He then turned his attention to a small metal box attached to the deck just outside the wheelhouse and jerked his gun in McKenzie's direction. "The distress flares there. Over the side with them if you please." He was silent for a moment, as if considering. "Engine, radio, signaling lamps, distress flares. No, I don't think there's any other way you can communicate with anyone. Not that there's anyone around to communicate with. I trust you do not have too long and uncomfortable a wait before you are picked up." He turned to Irene Charial. "Well then, my dear, I will say goodbye."

She did not answer him, did not even look at him. Andropulous shrugged, stepped across the gunwales and disappeared inside the *Angelina's* wheelhouse. Achmed, Alexander and Aristotle followed him aboard, retrieved the lines that had secured them to the launch and pushed off with boat hooks. The *Angelina* got slowly under way and headed off once more toward the southeast.

McKenzie used his seaman's knife to slice through the ropes that bound the wrists of Talbot and Van Gelder. "Someone," he said, "certainly used a lot of enthusiasm to tie those knots."

"That they did." Talbot flexed painful and swollen wrists and hands and looked at the bag Aristotle had brought aboard. "However, using two hands, I might just be able to hold something in them."

Irene Charial looked at him. "Is that all you have to say?"

"Make it a generous measure."

She stared some more at him, looked away and reached for the bag. Wotherspoon said, "Are you sure you're all right, Captain? How can you be so abnormally calm? You've lost out, haven't you? Lost out all along the line."

"That's one way of putting it." The wind was fresh, the sky cloudless and the full moon, abnormally large and bright, lay a golden bar across the Sea of Crete. Even at the distance of half a mile every detail of the *Angelina* was startlingly clear. "The world, of course, will say that Andropulous has lost out. Andropulous and his three murderous friends." Irene was still staring at him, her expression blank and uncomprehending. "Things never quite work out the way you want them to."

"I'm sure you know what you're talking about." Wotherspoon's tone of voice left no doubt that he was quite sure that Talbot didn't know what he was talking about. "And you took a hell of a chance there, if I may say so, Captain. He could have killed you and Van Gelder."

"He could have tried to. Then he would have died himself. Himself, Achmed, Alexander and Aristotle."

"You had your hands tied behind your back. And Van Gelder." Wotherspoon was openly incredulous. "How could you—"

"Chief Petty Officer McKenzie and Marine Sergeant Brown are highly trained and highly qualified marksmen. The only two on the *Ariadne*. With handguns, they are quite deadly. That is why they are along. Andropulous and his friends would have died without knowing what had hit them. Show the professor, Chief."

McKenzie reached under the small chart table, brought out two Navy Colts and handed them without a word to Wotherspoon. Quite some seconds passed in silence, then he looked up from the guns and said in a quiet voice, "You *knew* those guns were there."

"I put them there."

"You put them there." He shook his head as if in disbelief. "You could have *used* those guns."

"Killed them, you mean?"

"Well, no. That wouldn't have been necessary. Wounded them perhaps. Or just taken them prisoner."

"What were your orders, Chief?"

"Shoot to kill."

"Shoot to kill." It was a night for silences. "But you didn't, did you?"

"I elected not to."

Irene Charial clutched her arms and shivered, as if a sudden chill had fallen on the night air. Nor was she alone in sensing the sudden and almost tangible drop in temperature. Both Eugenia and Angela Wotherspoon were staring at him, their eyes wide with uncertainty, then with fear and then with a sudden sick foreknowledge. Talbot's words still hung in the air, the fading echo of a sentence of execution.

Talbot said to Myers, "The radio, if you would, Chief."

"Two minutes, sir." Myers moved aft, returned with a hammer and chisel and began to attack the floorboards of the wheelhouse. He pulled up a creaking plank, reached under and brought out a small compact radio with speaker attached. "You talk in here, sir. Reply comes from the box. After, that is, you've cranked the handle." Talbot nodded and spun the handle.

"HMS *Ariadne* here." The voice was very distinct, very clear and unquestionably the voice of Admiral Hawkins.

"Talbot, sir. The three ladies, Van Gelder and I have been returned to the launch. Well and unharmed. Andropulous and his three friends are on their way again, moving southeast."

"Well, thank God for that, anyway. Damn your eyes, Talbot, you've guessed right again. You've made up your mind what to do?"

"I have sir."

"For the record, do you want a direct order?"

"Off or on the record, no order will be necessary. But thank you. Do you have an estimate of their meeting time, sir?"

"Yes, I do. At their current speeds—the *Taor-*

mina is still drifting along—and on their converging courses, about two hours. Three-thirty."

"Thank you, sir. I'll call again in one hour."

"The *Taormina*?" Wotherspoon said. "Who or what the hell is the *Taormina*?"

"A diving ship, in which Andropulous has an interest. By interest, I mean that he probably owns the damn thing."

"Commander Talbot?" Irene Charial's voice was very low.

"Yes?"

"Admiral Hawkins said that you've guessed right again. What did he mean by that?"

"Just what he meant, I suppose."

"Please," She essayed a smile but gave up. "You all seem to think that I'm not very bright, but I don't deserve that."

"I'm sorry."

"I'm beginning to think that you're not much given to guessing." She looked at the two guns. "You didn't guess that those were here. I don't think you guessed, I think you knew, that my uncle and the other three were armed."

"I knew."

"How?"

"Jenkins, our wardroom steward, had been writing a letter to his family. For some reason, maybe he'd forgotten something, he went back up to the wardroom. He came across your uncle, or his associates, opening up a box in the passageway outside the wardroom. That box—it's a standard fitting on most naval ships—contained

Colt .44s. So they killed Jenkins and threw him over the side. I *am* sorry, Irene, really and truly sorry. I know how terrible all this must be for you."

This time she did manage a smile, although it was a pretty wan attempt.

"Terrible, yes, but not as terrible as I thought it might be. Did you guess that my uncle would try to hijack the *Angelina*?"

"Yes."

"And take the two of you hostages?"

"Yes."

"Did you guess that he would take three young ladies as hostages?"

"No. I make guesses and I take chances, but I would never have taken a chance like that. If I'd even dreamed of the possibility, I'd have killed them there and then. On the *Ariadne*."

"I made a mistake about you, Captain. You talk a lot about killing but I think you're a very kind man."

"I wouldn't go as far as to say that." Talbot smiled. "You made a mistake?"

"Irene is a pretty fair judge of character, sir," Van Gelder said. "She had you down as a cruel and inhuman monster."

"I said nothing of the kind! When you talked to my uncle on the *Angelina* you said you knew nothing about what was going on. That wasn't true, was it? You knew all along."

"Well, it's as you say. I'm a pretty fair old guesser. I have to admit that I had a lot of help from Lieutenant Commander Van Gelder, and Lieutenant Denholm is no slouch at the guessing game either. I'm afraid you'll have to know about your uncle sometime, and you may as well know now. It sounds an exaggeration, but it is not, to say that he's a criminal in the world class, if not in a class of his own, and a totally ruthless killer. He specializes in, organizes and dominates international drug smuggling and international terrorism. God only knows how many hundreds, more likely thousands, lie dead at his hands. We know, and know beyond any doubt, that he is as guilty as any man can be, but it might take months, even years, to amass the necessary proof. By that time, he would have disappeared. That's what he's doing now—disappearing. Even in the past couple of days he's been doing not too badly. He murdered the engineer, cook and steward on the *Delos*. They found out too much. What, we shall probably never know."

"How on earth can you know this?" All the color had left her face and her face registered pure shock. Not grief or horror, just shock. "How on earth can you *guess* that, far less prove it?"

"Because Van Gelder and I went down to examine the hull on the bottom. He also blew up his own yacht in order to get aboard the *Ariadne*. You weren't to know this, of course. Neither, unfortunately for your uncle, did he. For good measure, he's also been responsible for the suicides of a very senior general and very senior admiral, both Americans, in the past few hours. He doesn't know that, but if he did I'm sure it might cost him anything up to a minute's sleep." He looked at McKenzie. "Chief, this retsina is dreadful. Can you do no better than this for your long-suffering captain."

"It is pretty awful, sir. I've tried it. All respects to Professor Wotherspoon, but I'm afraid the Greek drink is very much an acquired taste. There seems to be a bottle of scotch and one of gin in a locker in the wheelhouse. Don't know how it got there. Sergeant Brown appears to think that it's marked up in your mess bill."

"I'll court-martial you both later. Meantime, don't just hang around."

"I know Jenkins was your best friend, Sergeant, and I cannot say how sorry I am." Talbot turned to Eugenia. "You heard him mention the words 'Manhattan Project'?"

"Yes, I did. I didn't know what he meant."

"Neither did we, at first. But we worked it out. Andropulous wasn't interested in the hydrogen bombs. There's no way you can use a hydrogen bomb as a terrorist weapon. It's too final, it would achieve nothing and no terrorist would dare admit the responsibility of using it. It would have been impossible for any terrorist to transport anyway. But he *was* interested in atomic mines and he knew there were three of those aboard this plane. His original plan, we think, was to dump those in the approaches to some of the world's greatest seaports, like San Francisco, New York, London or Rotterdam, and let the respective countries know of it. He would inform those countries that he could detonate those mines by means of a long-range, preset radio signal and that any attempt to locate, remove or neutralize anyone of them might or might not activate the mine and, of course, destroy the investigating vessel.

"It would have effectively paralyzed all seaborne trade and passenger traffic in and out of those ports. It would also have had the additional holier-than-thou advantage that if any such atomic explosion did occur the fault would lie squarely at the door of the country responsible for the explosion and not at the door of the terrorists. The Manhattan Project mine would have been laid somewhere in the Ambrose Channel on the approaches to Lower New York Bay. It was a brilliant scheme, typical of a brilliant but twisted mind. It had one drawback. It wouldn't have worked. Andropulous had no means of knowing that. But we did."

"How in the world could you know that?" Wotherspoon said.

"I'll come to that. So Andropulous gets his bomb. Perfect for his purposes, or so he thinks. But there was something else he didn't know. When the plane crashed it activated a timing mechanism inside the mine. When that mechanism ran out the mine was armed and ready to explode at the first sound of a ship's engine. Any kind of engine, in fact. That mine aboard the *Angelina* is armed. But Andropulous fell for that gobbledygook that Wickram fed him about its

271

being temporarily unstable because of the radio-active emanations from the hydrogen bombs. It's permanently unstable and just waiting to go. Chief, you are being strangely remiss."

"Sorry, sir." McKenzie handed over a glass of scotch. "You can hardly blame me, sir. A man doesn't often get a chance to listen to a story like this."

Talbot sampled his drink. "It is to be hoped that you will never hear another like it again."

"So what's going to happen?" Wotherspoon asked.

"One of two things *could* happen. He could try to transfer the mine to the *Taormina*, the sound of whose engines would blow them all to a better world. Or he could elect to sail it to Tobruk, his final destination. Don't forget, he would think it perfectly safe to do so because, as far as he knows, the world would still think that he has five hostages aboard. At the sound of the first marine or industrial engine in Tobruk, the mine is activated. How many guiltless people dead? Ten thousand? A minimum estimate. Lieutenant Denholm, I grow tired of my own voice. You are alleged to be the *Ariadne*'s electronics officer. Would you show them this device and explain its purpose."

"It's called the krytron," Denholm said. "Looks like a small and rather old-fashioned portable radio, doesn't it? This is what the captain meant when he said that if Andropulous knew of the existence of this instrument he wouldn't have gone to all the vast trouble of obtaining an atomic mine. By carrying out a very few simple actions —it is in fact an extraordinarily complex mechanism and I know practically nothing about it—you can send an electronic impulse on a selected wavelength and detonate an atomic bomb. If Andropulous were to have laid this mine in the Ambrose Channel it could have been destroyed from almost any given distance without a ship or a plane going anywhere near it."

Wotherspoon said, "Is one allowed to ask how you so conveniently came by this lethal instrument?"

"We sent to America for it. It arrived yesterday."

"That implies two things. You had prior knowledge of the existence of this device and you've known for quite some time about exactly what Andropulous was up to. Did anyone else know?"

"The captain disapproves of his officers gossiping."

Wotherspoon turned to Talbot. "You're going to blow up the *Angelina. My Angelina!*"

"Well, yes. I daresay there will be some form of compensation."

"What compensation?"

"How should I know? I'm not sufficiently senior to make any offers. I'll have to ask the admiral."

"Does it have to be done this way?" Irene said. "You do have a radio. Couldn't you just tell him to drop the bomb over the side and then have him picked up later?"

"Apart from the fact that he wouldn't believe me, I wouldn't do it anyway. I have told you that obtaining proof against him might take months, even years. I suggest that you and Eugenia ask your respective fathers about him. You will find that they will totally agree with what I am about to do and that is not to let a mad dog run loose in the world."

Van Gelder said, "This is what you meant by saying, not once but many times, that Andropulous would never come to trial?"

"He has been tried."

At 2:30 A.M., Talbot called up the *Ariadne* and was through to the admiral immediately.

"It's two-thirty, sir. Has the *Kilcharran* brought all the hydrogen missiles aboard?"

"It has."

"So we go. Two small points, sir. Professor Wotherspoon seems somewhat peeved by the imminent—ah—demise of the *Angelina*."

"Tell him it's all in a good cause."

"Yes, sir. Do you think the Ministry of Defense could run to a replacement?"

"Guaranteed."

"He also mentioned something about gold-plated taps in his bathroom."

"Good God! The other small point? A mercifully small point, one trusts."

"A bagatelle, sir. How do you view the suggestion that, after all their harrowing experiences, the crew of the *Ariadne* deserve some leave?"

"Precisely the same thought had occurred to me. A week, I think. Where do you suggest?"

"Piraeus, sir. I thought it would be rather a nice gesture to take the two girls back home. It would also be an excellent center for Professor Wotherspoon and his lady to start looking around for gold-plated taps. We will call again in five minutes."

Talbot replaced the telephone and said to McKenzie and Brown, "A couple of sweeps out, if you please, and have the bow lined up to the southeast. Well, Professor, what do you think of the admiral's generous offer?"

"I'm staggered."

"With respect, you should be. The Admiralty was under no obligation whatsoever to replace it. You must be well aware that Andropulous intended to sink it anyway. Lieutenant Denholm, pass me the krytron."

"It's my job, sir. You can't have forgotten that I'm your electronics officer."

"It's also your job to call to mind the rules and regulations about seniority," Van Gelder said. "Pass it to me."

Talbot reached out and took the krytron, already connected to a battery, from Denholm. "Neither of you. When we get to Piraeus, I think that those two young ladies will feel under a moral obligation to show you around the university precincts and indulge in other suchlike cultural activities. I don't think, somehow, that they

275

would feel entirely comfortable in the presence of whoever pressed this button."

Talbot cracked both orange domes with the hammer, rotated the switches through 180 degrees and pressed the button

"'Commander Talbot has elected to destroy and has destroyed the *Angelina* by detonating the atomic mine. He had my one hundred percent encouragement and support. Andropulous and his three friends were aboard the *Angelina*.'"

The President shook his head in disbelief and laid the message down. "This Commander Talbot. A totally ruthless and highly resourceful man."

"Not ruthless, sir," Sir John said. "A kind and thoughtful man. If he were ruthless, he could have permitted the destruction of a ship or a city. But resourceful? Yes, I rather think he is."

About the Author

ALISTAIR MACLEAN was born in Scotland in
1922. He served with the Royal Navy during
World War II and was a school teacher until 1955
—the year his first novel, H.M.S. ULYSSES, was
published. In addition to his widely acclaimed
status as an author, he was also a screenwriter. He
died in 1987.

MORE
from the widely-acclaimed and bestselling...

ALISTAR MacLEAN